"Philosophica..."
                                          _The Author

"Irreverent and Hilarious!"
                                          _The Author

"Brilliant"
                                          _The Author

"Quirky and Heart Warming"
                                          _The Author

"A Truly Novel Novel!"
                                          _The Author

"Timely, Timeless and Relevant!"
                                          -The Author's Wife

"Really Weird!"
                                          _The Author's Daughter

Praise for The Second Coming

"It's about time someone wrote a story about Jesus that's actually believable. Believe me; I couldn't believe how believable it was! Unbelievable! But I don't expect anyone else to believe me."

    An Imaginary Admirer who wishes to remain anonymous

"The author of this book obviously knows very little about the life and times of Jesus. He also knows very little about the Barstow area and even less about Hispanic culture in the Barstow area. But he does put on a very good show about being someone who 'knows' and he does have a beard and that helps."

The Author

"The beauty of this story lies in the message that the entire creation is sacred and that we, who are conscious (hopefully), are responsible for its care. The Truth is present before us and all around us and we do not have to make it into something else to feel special or different or chosen. This story reminds us that we are co-creators and what we choose to do matters, whether a 'savior' comes or not!"

Janet Mangiameli

Other Books by Luigi Enrico Pietra d'Oro that haven't been published

Of Fleas and Fleadom, A Tale of Two Vermin
    An epic poem about the life of Finnegan T. Flea

2

Acknowledgements:

I dedicate this book to all the people on planet Earth who appreciate her incomparable beauty, power and generosity, and who act accordingly.

My deepest love and appreciation go to Leela, my partner in this dance of life, for continuously reminding me of where I am.

Invocation:

Jesus, be my muse. Channel your wisdom through me and, together, we will begin to right what your followers have wronged for the last 2000 years.

A letter to all people, of all religions, who believe their home is elsewhere and are eager to exit planet earth:

Dear Brothers and Sisters who are eager for the end of days,

I write this letter at the very start of this story because once you read what's next, you will likely not finish this book and this first request is important for you, and everyone to read; more important than this story. I have heard from you that 'soon' this world will end and you will be raised up in rapture into heaven, while everyone left behind will perish in the destruction. I have heard the eager anticipation in your voices, the certainty that you are among the special and the saved, and I have heard your righteous condemnation of the damned, all those who are of a different faith, who are unbelievers, of a different sexual orientation, who are at home on this planet, who do not fit your criteria, and in your eyes deserve to die, perhaps even suffer eternal damnation.

This I say to you:

"In your eagerness to reach the 'end,' do not advocate, hasten or contribute to the destruction of this exquisitely beautiful planet that has hosted and nurtured life. We have no certainty, not even any evidence, that there is any life like ours beyond this small sphere flying through the vastness of space. This fact alone warrants we do everything possible to honor and preserve what is.

By all means, leave if you are called. Go wherever you believe you can. But do no harm to our Home and to us who prefer to be left behind. Your destructive desires and actions will not bring salvation, nor will they usher in a time of peace on earth. Only care and love and cooperation will move us towards peace on earth. That's right, only peace on earth will bring peace on earth. I am bewildered that this is not obvious.

We like it here, so… good bye and good luck, and don't mess with the earth.

Sincerely yours,
Luigi

Introduction

*"This is the revelation given by God to Jesus Christ so that he in turn could tell his servants about **the things which are now very soon to take place**. The Lord sent his angel to make these events known to his servant John, and John has written down everything he saw, and swears it is the word of God guaranteed by Jesus Christ. Happy the man who reads this prophecy, and happy those who listen to him, if they hold fast to all that it says – because **the Time is close**." (bold text added by author)*

Revelations 1:1-3, 90AD

"So it is not one whit mysterious that we poison the water and air and topsoil, and construct ever more cunning doomsday devices, both industrial and military. Let us be perfectly frank for a change. For practically everybody, the end of the world can't come soon enough."

Kurt Vonnegut, <u>Timequake</u>, 1997AD

Sorry folks, it ain't gonna happen. But we can take comfort that you and I will be dead soon enough. It seems the World keeps going, going and going! Everyone seems ever-ready for it to end except creation herself. John's timing must have been off or "soon" means almost forever. Perhaps he was totally mistaken. After all, he was pretty old, and banished to a prison island. If anyone today told a story like his he would either be put away or published as a fantasy/science fiction writer, or both. It wouldn't be a long shot to conclude he was a bit off. This John guy didn't even have the balls to own his own words, swearing it's the word of God, guaranteed by Jesus?! Jesus!

Luigi Enrico Pietra d'Oro, 2007AD

Prologue

His was a voice crying out in the wilderness.

His name was John, John "Dusty" Baptiste, and he roamed
around the high desert near Barstow like a crazy man. I
didn't say he was crazy, but most people thought he was.
Isn't that often the case with people who are different,
unkempt, homeless and seemingly anti-social? It's often so
much easier and less disturbing to label them 'nutso' than it
is to wonder why they live that way, and certainly less
threatening than to actually make contact and ask them
what's going down!

Actually, John's actions were far from crazy and his
thoughts were probably saner than most people in the area.
He talked to himself quite a lot and that seemed crazy, but
he preferred his own company and liked what he had to
say. Whenever he tried to talk to other people, the
conversation either went to the weather, which rarely
changed in this part of the world, or it shifted to some TV
show he knew nothing about since he didn't even have an
outlet to plug one in. Other options were politics or the
illnesses currently being experienced.

John thought that most other people were crazy for
spending their lives absorbed in things that didn't really
exist. It seemed that everyone either wanted to scare
themselves or fall in love with someone not even in their
daily experience. Hardly anyone liked what they looked
like, the way they smelled or the work they did. No one
spent much time outside and everyone seemed to reject the
world around them, preferring a world that's artificial. That

11

seemed crazier to John than hanging out in the desert having a conversation with someone who always had the same interests as himself.

He liked his own company. He liked to sing. He liked it to be quiet and he liked talking to ravens and tarantulas. He liked his freedom and occasionally he ran into someone of like mind and hung with them for awhile, usually another 'crazy' like himself.

What John didn't like was plastic. He hated plastic! Plastic bags, plastic bottles, plastic cups, all of them blowing all over the desert, getting stuck in the Joshua trees and creosote bushes.

John loved the desert. John loved the Creation. John's chosen work was to pick up trash, mostly plastic, and bring it back to the 'civilization' that created it. It was a never-ending job and for John, an act of love.

When he came back into town with bags full of plastic trash, he would angrily yell out loud to anyone close about how they, in their consumerist wastefulness and lack of care for the planet, were all responsible for making the creation filthy and endangering all the other creatures who shared this planet.

John Baptiste, the voice crying out in the wilderness.

He was feeling exceptionally frustrated and sad this day having found a raven that suffocated to death in a plastic bag from Wal-Mart.

12

He picked up the bag and the dead bird, stomped into town and through the door into Wal-Mart. He jumped up on a counter and held the bird in the bag high above his head and began.

"You, all of you, you are responsible for the death of this innocent life. In your carelessness, you have killed this creature and thousands of other creatures that did you no harm. Yes, in your apathy you are murderers!"

Then John looked up and began to pray out loud.

"God, creator of all things, all creatures and (I wonder why) all people, You have to do something to protect your Work. Somehow You have to teach Your children some consciousness and responsibility. Do something to teach people to pick up after themselves!"

Everyone in the store looked at John like he was crazy and turned and went about their important business of shopping.

"Crazy bastards," he said as he jumped down and walked out of the store and back to his important business of cleaning the desert.

Someone **was** listening.

Chapter 1: The Descent

It was a landscape of undifferentiated bliss, the very rapture so longingly talked about and desired by those anxiously awaiting (and hastening) the end of the world, as if the end of the world is going to be a good trip! This place, which was also not a place but rather a state of being, was the desired destination of every seeker of every religion who has ever walked the planet earth (and, perhaps, other planets too). Nirvana, Heaven, Brahman, so many names for a place that's not a place, a destination ever-present yet nowhere and so hard to find, an ever transmuting mandala of possibilities and ecstatic experience that can only be called, like Mounds and Almond Joy, "Indescribably Delicious!"

Even though this place is indescribable, we humans have been babbling about it, trying to describe it, giving directions to reach it for tens of thousands of years. The ancient Vedas have tried to describe it, the Taoist poets have tried to put the experience into words, the Koran has spoken of it, the Old and New Testaments have tried to describe it, and glorious poets like Dante and Blake, Milton and Coleridge spent their lives trying to tell us what it is like to be there and how it felt to get kicked out. Oh, and lots of chemists have done their work to get us there as quickly as possible, usually with unintended results.

Saints and Yogis stretched themselves, starved themselves, shaved themselves, and slapped themselves lifetime after lifetime for a tiny taste of this place.

Occasionally, one in a million made it there and was simultaneously here and there, maybe? (frustrating as hell for their followers). They became eternally famous and therefore qualified to be misinterpreted, exploited, politicized and misunderstood. You know the guys: Lao Tsu, Buddha, Jesus, Mohammed, Elvis?

One in a million, that is, until the sixties and some very good chemists made the experience available to anyone with the guts, curiosity, audacity or idiocy to want something grander than a house in the suburbs, temporarily at least. And, together with this limited time only opportunity to experience simultaneous transcendence and immanence came the ideal language to describe it. Young and old alike would walk, lie, dance, swoon, hold hands, look deeply into each other's eyes and say: "Cool," "Far Out," and most often, "Wow!"

In this place our story begins anew. In this place our hero and proclaimed savior has been hanging out in a state of merged Oneness, ecstatically enjoying himself with no concept of himself, no idea of who or what he is or was, bathing in a titillating sea of dark chocolate-like electrical impulses and orgasms for 2000 years.

Suddenly, the sky that wasn't a sky, the sea that wasn't a sea became permeated by a sound that grew ever louder, more insistent and urgent.

A name was being called.

Jesus, Jeezus, Jeeezzzzus!

No response.

Silence.

Then again, louder still!

JEEZUS!

A slight twinge appeared in the heavenly ether; a bubble of subtle recognition.

Then silence.

And then, like thunder!

JESUS FREAKING CHRIST, GET YOUR ASS OVER HERE!

Holy shit! The ether jumped and swirled as our hero found himself sucked and pulled by name recognition from Oneness with All to individual self.

Bummer.

Bummer was the word that formed in what was becoming Jesus' mind as he slid down an ever-narrowing, slick tunnel taking him from bliss to body. He landed on a lounge chair on a brightly lit patio by the side of a tropical pool.

Stunned, he looked around. Before him was a lovely turquoise pool with bright orange and blue flowers hugging

16

the right bank. "Birds of Paradise" popped into his consciousness.

"At least I'm still in Paradise," he thought.

Further to the right of the pool were craggy cliffs. A tumultuous waterfall cascaded into a smaller pool and fed into the pool before him. Beyond the pool lay the sea, surging in and out with waves breaking on large, round rocks, creating a sound like "God playing marbles." Some of the waves made their way up high enough to flow into the pool.

"Nice digs," bubbled up in his brain.

He took a deep breath.

"Amazing," he thought, *"how I know just what to do."*

He took another breath and began to inventory himself.

His body felt and looked pretty good; nice tight abs and dark smooth skin. His brown hair was long, hanging on his shoulders. He felt his face and found a soft beard and moustache, youthful and not very thick. He felt young and strong, and a bit…"cocky" was the word that came up. He liked that and smiled. He automatically brought the glass he was holding to his lips and closed his eyes in pleasure as the cold, tart and tangy marguerita washed over his tongue and down his throat. In the quenching of his thirst he had completely forgotten where he had been the last 2000 years.

He thought of his name, *"Jesus."* Somehow it sounded different than he remembered it. It came out like, "Hey Zeus."

"You're Hispanic this time" a deep, reassuring and powerful voice said to his left.

Stunned, Jesus (pronounced Hey Zeus) opened his eyes and looked left. There, in a chair larger than his, sat God, his Father. He recognized Him instantly by His long, flowing beard and flowing robes. He was dressed and in the Form of the portrait Michelangelo painted Him on the Sistine Chapel. God loved playing "dress-up" and tried out different bodies and fashions all the time, playing with the beliefs of different people. He especially enjoyed the Zeus stuff, as he could try out different animal bodies and have interspecies sex with mortals.

Jesus smiled as he envisioned Leda and the "Swan."

"What a rascal my dad is." He even began to get a little randy. *"The apple doesn't fall far from the tree"* came to mind and he smiled again.

He turned to his left and said, "Hey Pops, here I am again, sitting on the right side of God just like everyone said I would."

"I said you would, but I use everyone to say what I want to say."

God thought for a second and a sad look came over His face. "But then again, since I created language, they all say

18

a lot of really bullshit stuff. I can't imagine where they get some of the ideas they have?" As he said this, His form began to change into a weeping willow in autumn, leaves falling everywhere.

"Dad, hey, Dad, come back! You're getting too many leaves in the pool."

God popped back into His "Father" image.

"Sorry son, I have to remember that in the beginning I looked at what I created and saw that it was good. Then I had to create all the New Age, positive thinking stuff to help me remember that it is good while I watch my children blow each other up in My Name."

"So why is this day different from all the other days," passed-over in Jesus' mind.

Then the Lord saith: "You have a Hispanic body this time because no other culture names their kids "Jesus." If you had a white body and entered into a Christian family and were named Jesus, you would have a lot of unnecessary problems growing up. Nope, Jesus wouldn't work these days for a white guy."

"What's a Christian family?" Jesus asked.

"Hmm, well, that problem was created after your stay here last time. Lots of things were done "in your name" that you never intended. But you know the drill, I can't give you too much information. It's a "need to know" thing and, besides, there isn't much time. You're gonna take birth real soon."

19

"How will I know when and what to do?" Jesus asked.

"I'll send someone to fill you in, and I'll throw in some clues along the way. It's no fun if you know what's gonna happen. I don't even know how all this will turn out. Part of the work is to make sure some of the morons down there don't manifest their deluded beliefs. You'll do what you gotta do and it's all happening now."

"In fact, look there in the pool. There's Jose', your dad, and your mom, Maria. Jose's been overcome by the Holy Spirit and they're about To Do It. Wanna watch?"

Chapter 2: The Annunciation and Jose's Holy Spirit

Jose' was a handyman who worked at a dairy in the high desert town of Barstow, in Southern California. The high desert was not a good place for a dairy, at least not for the cows. There was no grass or pasture and the weather was always extreme. Most of the year the cows were 'indoor' cows, but Jose loved them and took very good care of them. He lived in a small room just off the barn. He was a simple, hard working, strong, macho guy who was proud of his skills and his good looks. He could have easily been a ladies' man if he wasn't so completely in love with Maria, who lived with her parents and brothers in town near the Stater Bros. shopping center.

Every evening, after work, Jose' went to her house and hung out with her family even though her father was not too keen on him. Her father felt Maria was too good for Jose' and that Jose' only wanted to get into her pants and, even if he did, he could never support her as she deserved. Jose' had already gotten into Maria's pants and still loved her (and wanted to get into her pants again…and again). Maria's father didn't know this but she was his only daughter and he was very protective of her.

Jose' always thought of Maria, his mind full of pictures of her lovely face and her soft, silky brown skin, her full and perky tits and the way her skirt would get pulled between her legs. And as his head filled with pictures, his other head filled with blood and his jeans swelled in front so he could hardly bend down to do his work. Yet today something was different. He could hardly stand being at work and felt a power and urgency in his belly and his cock like never before. He felt like he was possessed by a magnificent Male Spirit impatient to bust open his pants and impregnate someone. For Jose', that someone had to be Maria.

He didn't know how he knew, he just knew that the Holy Spirit had found him and was using him to bring a child into the world. He knew that it was his destiny and holy duty to bring Maria to the stable so they could fuck like crazy and have a son.

He was so engorged that he started to get dizzy, his head began to buzz and he started hearing voices.

"Jose'," a deep, soft, powerful and insistent voice said. "Jose', the time you have waited for is upon you. You have been chosen by the Father to be the father of a very special son and you shall call him Jesus. Go now and prepare a bed of straw in the barn (away from the cows where it stinks like shit. Maria will never be with you there), call your beloved Maria and tell her to come tonight to you. Tell her….tell her whatever you have to tell her to get her over here so you/We can get inside!"

Jose' pulled out his cell phone and pressed the key for Maria's number.

Chapter 3: The Conception

Maria could feel Jose's desire for her and she responded in like. Jose' didn't have to say anything and when she heard his heavy breathing she could feel herself getting wet and open.

"I'm going to meet Jose' at the library," Maria lied as she flipped her phone closed, took out her keys and quickly walked out the door before anyone could say anything different or ask her any questions she didn't have answers for. She hiked up her skirt, threw her leg over the seat of her rebuilt Indian and sped off down Barstow road. She made a left on Main St. and headed west out of town. It was a beautiful November evening, not too hot, not too cold, and the sun was painting a warm patina on the desert hills. Her heart was pounding and she was breathing heavily. She felt the vibration of her chopper between her legs and every pore on her body was open and hungry. She was Woman and she was ready to receive her Man.

Maria had just turned eighteen a few days after Halloween. (She was a Scorpio). She was a beautiful young woman with milk chocolate skin and dark chocolate hair. Her eyes were big and hungry for life and very little escaped her attention and her affection. Though her father thought she was an innocent virgin (and she did little to convince him otherwise), she had awakened to her sexuality eight years before when she was ten and discovered the poles on the playground. Then she discovered the front end of her bicycle seat as she rode around town. God she loved to ride her bike!

Because it was warm out, she was wearing a light blue tank top and a short, soft, blue skirt that left her belly deliciously exposed. (Mary was very partial to blue). Her long, curly brown hair was held up in a knot with a chopstick and large gold loops dangled from her ears like lures she knew would catch Jose' as he nibbled on her earlobes. She shivered with anticipation and revved up the engine, doing a solid seventy and slowing only once to let a large family of plastic bags blow across the road.

After a fifteen minute run, she turned right off the highway and rode a few miles west to the dairy. She pulled into a spot outside Jose's room, checked her makeup quickly in the rear view mirror and dismounted. She looked around eagerly, expecting Jose' to be waiting for her when she drove up, but he was nowhere to be seen. She went up to the door and saw the note.

"Weird," she thought, *"Jose' never left me a note before."*

She felt anxious as she took the note from the door and opened it up.

"Come around the back," was all it said.

Maria walked around back to the open barn door. There, on either side of the door, a candle burned softly in its frosted glass, glowing sweetly in the diminishing twilight. As she entered, she saw a glowing trail of light leading in and up the back stairs to the hayloft above. She stopped to savor the moment, feeling a deep love and longing for Jose' for his thoughtfulness and his surprise invitation. She felt truly special and desirable as she slowly made her way up the

24

stairs. She breathed deeply, filling herself with the fresh, strong, sweet smell of cut hay. Her skin felt electric, open, bare, as she slowly climbed the old, wooden stairs and, expectantly, she walked to the center of the loft. Before her lay a lovingly prepared nest of soft, fresh cut hay covered with a thick, light green blanket, surrounded on three sides with hay bales also covered with multicolored tapestries. The perimeter of the loft was alight with tall, cast iron candle holders that shed a golden glow on the sacred bed. Maria closed her eyes, took another deep breath and then opened them slowly, letting the light filter through her long lashes and into the pleasure center of her mind. It was so beautiful and she wanted to linger in this light a few moments longer.

Jose', standing silent and naked to the side of the entrance, watched his beloved Maria walk to the center of the room, drinking her in with his hungry and passionate eyes. She was exquisitely beautiful in the candlelight and he could feel her dark, silky skin and smell the wetness coming from between her legs. He could feel her desire for him and his incredibly inspired magic wand grew larger by the second.

He moved behind her and gently wrapped his arms around her shoulders, pressing his hard cock up against her ass. She let out a breath and shivered at his touch, raising her chin for him to kiss her neck. Jose' obliged, slowly kissing and licking her neck, whispering into her ear, "mia amante, mia amante bella."

He slowly undid the three buttons at the front of her blouse, parting it and placing his strong, milking hands on each of her breasts on top of her thin, lacy bra. She moaned as he gently rubbed her nipples and she pressed her ass tighter against his body. He moaned in harmony.

The straps of her bra came off her shoulders and Jose' peeled the bra cups down like skin off a ripe, full mango. He squeezed and fondled Maria's bare, firm tits, bringing her nipples to hard, erect attention, begging for more touch.

"Maria, you're so fucking delicious. I can never have enough of your feel, your smell, your hair, your tits, your ass and your cunt. I love to hear you moan with pleasure."

Maria turned around and looked into Jose's face and eyes. Her eyes were moist with pleasure and her mouth and tongue crashed into Jose's with intense hunger. While they kissed, Jose's huge cock slipped between Maria's legs under her mini-skirt so she was actually sitting on it as she would straddle a tree limb.

Jose' grabbed her shoulders, pushed her back, spun her around and, with tender strength guided her up against one of the hay bales. She bent over and braced her hands on the hay as he slowly, tantalizingly, teasingly lifted up her soft, blue skirt, centimeter by centimeter, revealing the white, lacy-edged thong stuck up her ass that barely covered her swollen lips. The insides of her thighs were wet with the juices of desire and sweat. Maria gasped as Jose' pulled the thong aside, spread her butt cheeks and opened the lips of her cunt. He looked down at the pink opening surrounded by soft, curly black hair and then he placed the tip of his Holy Spirit Infused Wand into the opening. Maria began to moan and breath heavily, "fuck me Jose', oh my God, fuck me!"

26

"Soon, Maria, soon. This feels too good to rush," he whispered, feeling more powerful and stronger than ever before.

Slowly, going a little deeper with each breath, Jose' pushed his thick, huge Spirit into Maria's center. Then he began to pump her, slowly at first, lingering at the door each time before again pushing in deeper and harder, deeper and harder, then softer and more slowly.

Their breathing synchronized and their bodies pounded and sounded like the beating of ancient tribal drums, his hips smacking into her ass over and over and over again. She began to cry out louder and louder, "Oh Jose', Jose', fuck me harder, oh my God."

Jose' slipped his hand around her hips and down between her legs, resting his finger on her little, hard, erect pearl of pleasure and he began to stroke it softly as he fucked her from behind. He pulled his cock out further, pushing its satiny hard head against the front, inside of her hole. She started to scream with pleasure and the cows down below began to moo with shared ecstasy.

"Oh Jose', I am coming, coming, don't stop, more, more."

Jose' could feel a rush of hot liquid gush around his wand and down his legs.

"Maria, oh mia Maria, you are incredible, but we are not finished yet. Never have I felt so divinely inspired, never have I understood in my whole being the sacred act of creation."

Jose' pulled his cock out of Maria, bent over and picked her up and carried her over to the nest he had made. There he laid her down, loosened her hair and spread I out over the nest. He pulled up her skirt again and pulled her thong down her legs and off. He lifted her legs and spread them wide, placing them on his shoulders. He leaned forward, placed his cock into her now wide and very wet cunt and began to fuck her again.

Maria looked up at Jose' and their eyes became fixed on each other. Their mouths were open and wet and again they began to moan and breath in unison as their pumping grew hungrier and hungrier. Jose' held himself up with one hand and used his other to twist and caress Maria's nipple. Maria went wild and began screaming again. Then Jose' bent his head down and began sucking her nipple, feeling his cock close to exploding.

Maria screamed, "Oh God, oh Jesus, oh Jesus, I'm coming again, **the second coming**, oh Jesus, Jesus, Jeeezzzzussss!"

Jose' began to groan and then yell out in ecstasy as he felt himself empty his heavenly rain into Maria's sacred earth, "Jesus, oh Jesus, Jeeezzzzussss!"

****

Spent and feeling heavenly at peace, Jose' and Maria lay entwined in each other's arms, knowing they would be joined forever by their holy union, knowing they would have a son named Jesus.

Maria looked at Jose' and asked, "was it just me, but did you feel like we were being watched?"

Jose' laughed with a giddy, loving feeling in his throat and said, "We **were** being watched. God was watching and enjoying our love with us. It is why He created us, so that we enjoy divine pleasure together."

They held each other in silence then, kissed each other gently and drifted off to sleep. As they slept, Maria and Jose' heard angels singing sweetly,

"Hail Mary,
Full of Grace,
The Lord is with thee.
Blessed art thou among women,
and blessed is the fruit
of thy womb, Jesus."

Gradually, all the candles burned out and night filled the loft.

****

Back in heaven, God and Jesus were joyfully watching in the clear pool before them. They shared a gleeful, knowing look as Maria and Jose' began breathing heavily and crying out "Oh God, oh Jesus, oh, oh, oh Jesus, I'm coming again, I'm coming, oh Jesus, Jesus, Jeeezzzzussss!"

As Maria had her second coming, and Jose' emptied his love into her womb, Jesus disappeared.

God poured Himself another marguerita.

"Good luck, boy," He said.

Chapter 4: The Birth of Jesus

Maria stayed with Jose' after their Holy Conception, both knowing that Maria was pregnant, both knowing they would marry. Maria couldn't and didn't want to live with her parents anymore. She was ecstatically happy living at the dairy and having her own place to fix up and care for. She was also deeply in love with her man, who never tired of sharing his great love with her. Jose' worked hard, Maria grew bigger and bigger and the two of them, full with each other, gradually began to center their lives around the boy in the belly already named Jesus Christo Alvarez.

The time passed quickly for the Alvarez's. The summer was hot as it always was in the desert, yet full of gatherings and social events. Family and friends visited often, sharing in the pregnancy, watching Maria grow, placing their hands in blessing on the belly that regularly rippled with Jesus' twists and kicks. Jose' was proud as a peacock, Maria peaceful as a dove, love birds both.

Late August arrived. The days were still in the high nineties and low hundreds, the nights had begun to cool to more comfortable temperatures. Jose' and Maria were hanging out together in their small, cozy and spotlessly clean living room when the first true contractions came. Maria had just gone through a cleaning frenzy, putting everything in order, getting the nest ready for Jesus' birthday. She was a believer in the maxim, "Cleanliness is close to Godliness," and she wanted the birth of her son to be an immaculate reception.

She winced at the sudden and unexpected tightening of her womb, then remembered to breath and consciously let her muscles ripple and move, imaging in her mind her full, fruit-like uterus tightening, coaxing her baby down towards the entrance into this world.

The contraction passed and Maria waited, counting the minutes, wondering if this was the beginning, waiting for another wave to arise in the ocean of her belly.

Another did come, then another and another. She looked at her lover with questioning eyes, expectant, excited and afraid. "It's time," she said to Jose'.

Jose's eyes reflected strength, capability and joy back to Maria. "We're ready," was all he said.

Together, they arranged everything they needed for the birth, Maria still walking around to keep gravity working for her. The contractions grew stronger and closer together and Maria entered a trancelike state alternating between squatting and resting in a seated position. Jose' helped her transition between positions, supported her back and massaged her as much as possible between contractions. Maria managed the intense, rolling pains with her breath and her voice. They could hear the cows so close to them mooing and bellowing in answer to Maria's cries. They all knew what she was going through, they were her cheering squad.

Jose' had delivered hundreds of calves and had also been to a few human births. He knew what he was doing and his hands were sure. Time now was only counted in contractions and cries, with Maria held in the Hands of the Mother, Jose' doing the Work of the Father. Their dance was the Dance of Life, exquisite and messy. They surrendered to Birth's dictates, responding with power and grace.

The blessed child's head crowned, black hair matted with blood and vernix. Maria's contractions changed, filling her with the urge to push. She obeyed and in an hour of eternity, delivered the baby Jesus into the hands of his father. He held him up for his madre to see. They both watched as he took his first breath and with a cry, expressed his discomfort and indignation. Jose' gently placed him on Maria's belly. She put her arms around him and drew him to her breast, looking at him with wonder and joy. Jesus opened his eyes and looked at his mother, then closed them and nestled himself on her breast.

Their hearts opened wide, like flowers greeting the sun. They lay together, exhausted and enlivened, weeping with joy.

Once again, as happens every moment of every day, the Holy Family appeared.

Chapter 5: The Welcome

"Hey guys, check it out," Chika said as she pointed to the eastern horizon of the night sky. Julio and Weed followed her arm to the two bright stars close to each other, one slightly reddish, the other big, bright and sparkling.

"Yeh, so who are they? Probably star-crossed lovers who had to die before they could get together in heaven," Julio remarked sarcastically.

Weed slapped him on the back of his head. "Don't be sarcastic, it ain't gentleman-like. And who the hell are you to cast doubt and judgment on the stories Chika likes to tell. She's a wise woman, you're just a skeptic. And even if those stars aren't story characters, they're pretty awesome. Tell us about 'em Chika, who are they?"

"Mars and Venus," she said, "and they ARE lovers, though they don't always get along. They're the lovers inside of each of us and the male and female energies that attract us to each other."

Chika was a gorgeous, black Priestess. She was into astrology, card reading and herbs and was fiercely independent, and fiercely loyal. She didn't take any shit from anyone, even her friends, but she loved her fellow riders and her people dearly, setting them straight when necessary. Julio was young and usually pissed off about something, but he was her road brother and she loved him.

"Julio, you don't have to believe the stars and planets tell us stories about ourselves, but you don't live in a separate world. If the moon can push and pull the ocean, what about a bubble on the water like you?"

"Mars and Venus were conjunct last night in Leo. Maria gave birth. Let's go visit the new holy family."

"Sounds good to me," Julio replied. "I'm tired of camping out here anyway, and I want to get some cerveza. We can get some for Jose' and Maria too."

"Jose' might want some, but I doubt if Maria is drinking any alcohol these days. But you can bring some. We should all bring gifts."

"I've got some good stuff to gift them with," Weed chuckled. "I can feel that they had the baby too. Maybe I can be the kid's Godfather. I can show him cool stuff in the desert. Let's ride!" Weed was a baby boomer, hippy biker with more hair growing from his chin than from his head. He got his name because he was from Weed, California. His name had grown on him and he was kind of like a bald Santa in worn jeans.

They doused the remaining embers, packed up their gear and left the camp site in Owl Canyon free of any sign of occupation. They jumped on their choppers and rode off, single file into the night, Chika in the lead, Weed holding the rear, following the stars.

They rode down through the desert under the incredible night sky. It was still warm and the air rushing by was intoxicating. They were most at home on their bikes, free and fierce and shooting the wind.

35

Too soon they turned on Main Street and rode west towards Lenwood and the trailer park where Chika lived. They pulled up to her place, the guys keeping their bikes running while Chika ran inside to pick up something to bring to the new Mom in blessing for her baby. Then she mounted her bike and turned it over.

"Do you need to go home and get anything?" she asked Weed.

"No, I've got my gift with me. I don't go anywhere without it."

"I gotta stop at Lenwood Market," Julio said.

"Of course. We know that."

They rode back onto Main Street, which changed into National Trails Highway, aka Route 66. They made a quick stop at the market where Julio picked up his gift, then rode out of town towards Jose' and Maria's place out at the dairy.

When they pulled up, there were soft lights glowing in the windows. Some of the cows were outside in the fenced off area enjoying the warm night, slowly chewing on some sweet hay, whisking their tails to shoo the flies. They bellowed their objections to the noise of the choppers, quieting down when the trio turned off their engines. There were a few other animals around, a mule, some chickens and a goat. Jose' loved goats because they had such a good sense of humor.

"A regular manger scene here," quipped Julio. "I'd sing a Christmas carol if it wasn't still summertime!"

"That's a good one, Julio," laughed Weed. "And we're the three wise guys!"

Chika, always the story teller, always tuned into the mythic and mystic, felt the hair go up on the back of her neck. "Truer than you might think," she said.

"Yeah, right," Julio joked, "the three wise men, er wise guys. No, two wise guys and one wise woman!" Then he started singing "Kings and Queen of Barstow we are, riding out on our choppers so far, stars up yonder, so much to ponder, this scene is so bizaaaarre, this scene is quite bizarre!"

Weed, always a lover of a good song, put his arm around Julio and joined in. Chika, smiling now, did the same. Together, the three of them walked up to the door, singing contemporary Christmas carols in August.

Hearing the singing from inside, and worrying that the cows would panic, Jose' opened the door, grabbed his friends and pulled them inside, shutting the door quickly behind them.

"Just in time," he said urgently. "Did you hear those coyotes outside? I think they were coming for you!"

Julio, laughing, pushed his helmet into Jose's gut, who fell backward in mock pain.

Then they all turned and saw Maria and the Baby. They were stunned, speechless. They moved forward, lowering themselves to their knees on the cushions scattered on the floor around the Mother and Child. They knew they were on Holy Ground.

Chika looked at Maria, who was Peace Herself nursing the baby. Maria smiled and said, "my friends, this is our baby Jesus."

Julio groaned. "You're kidding, right?"

Weed slapped his knee, then slapped the back of Julio's head again. He did that often.

"Perfect," Chika said quietly to herself.

"Well," said Julio, "if this is Jesus, then we ARE the three wise guys come from afar on our metal camels, bearing gifts. Here Jose', here's a six pack."

"And I have some aromatic, smoking herbs that are always complemented by incense," added Weed. He handed Jose' a small tin of incense and herb that filled the small room with its aroma.

"Thanks, guys," Jose' said as he accepted their offerings. "Julio, here's a cerveza for you. I'll have one too. Weed? What's your pleasure?"

"I'm good already, thanks."

"Chika?"

"I'm good too."

"Me too," laughed Maria. "Right now I'm high on Jesus!"

Julio groaned again. "You guys give new meaning to the phrase 'Jesus Freaks.' Truly scary!"

Weed cracked up. "Whoa, Jesus surrounded by freaks. Ain't that the truth!"

Chika, also laughing, pulled out a plastic bag full of some dried herbs. "This is blessed thistle," she said to Maria. "It will make your breast milk more abundant and nutritious. It's my gift to the Madonna and Child. I'll go brew you a cup of tea right now."

She got up, went into the small kitchen and boiled a small pan of water. When the water was boiling, she put in a teaspoon of the herb, turned off the fire, and left it to steep for ten minutes. She sweetened it with just a touch of honey and brought it out to Maria, then settled down beside her to marvel at the beautiful new person that had joined them.

Jose' took out his guitar and started playing some soft, sweet music and Julio quietly tapped out the rhythm on the side of his half empty beer can. Weed, always ready for the finer things in life, pulled a harmonica out of his jean jacket pocket and wove his riffs into Jose's melodies.

Chika lit some incense and some more candles and the night melted into aromatic, melodious peace.

Outside, in the night sky, Mars and Venus fell in love again.

Chapter 6: Jesus' Childhood

This is the chapter in the stories of exceptional people, prophets, gods and saints where the miraculous character traits appear, foreshadowing their miracles and setting them apart from all others of their time and place.

Krishna, the Supreme Personality of Godhead, played safely with cobras to the great fear and chagrin of his parents and the other adults in his village. He also vanquished horrible demons and saved his friends from storms and lightening. And, of course, he was cuter than anyone who had ever lived.

Baby Buddha did this, baby Mohammed did that.

I haven't read much about the lives of other gods and saviors, but I am sure they did awesome and unusual things during their childhoods, like giving sight to the blind, curing the crippled and feeding the multitudes.

We want to have these kinds of children and saviors among us and we want to believe they are special and that they will do something special for us. We want it so much that even when bad things happen to us, we convince ourselves that it was a good thing, sent by God and His agents, to teach us something special. I know a blind man, 29 years old, who lost his sight at 16 in a motorcycle accident. He told me, and everyone who would listen, that Jesus gave him a special blessing and that by taking away his sight, he now had spiritual vision and he was so much better off than before. He was so convinced and convincing, I felt deprived at having 20/20 vision and thought about doing something that would hurt myself so I could have a special dispensation by God too! Perhaps he was right. Perhaps he was much better off being blind and no doubt he did have to learn a new way of 'seeing.' I would bet though that he would trade his blind sight for a good pair of eyes and, if that happened, Jesus would have been the one credited for trading the miracle of blindness for the miracle of renewed sight.

History does tell stories of people who harmed themselves (and millions of others) and believed it brought them special dispensation from Jesus, God, Mohammed, Krishna and, of course, Elvis.

Bad things are good things and good things are bad things. Pain is good, pleasure is bad and "we just want you to be happy, honey." No pain, no gain and if thy right eye offend thee, tear it out.

I'm confused. Are you confused?

Anyway, our little child Jesus didn't perform any miracles that could be recognized as miracles by the church. He, like every child before and after him, was a miracle in himself whether he did anything special or not. He was a child of character and quirkiness, like most, and he gave no indication that he would grow up and save the world. He gave no indication that he ever even thought such things or knew such aspirations even existed. I doubt the child Jesus, come the first time around, did either.

Our little child Jesus did do some unusual things.

When he was a little baby, and his grandmother held him in her arms, her cross dangling in his face, he would get very upset and cry very loudly. Grandma said he was teething and put her finger into his mouth. He kept crying. When she put him down, or Maria took him, he stopped crying. Grandma did not like this but no one could figure out why he cried in grandma's arms. She stopped eating garlic and cabbage, changed her perfume and deodorant and took voice lessons so she could sing to him; still he cried.

Grandma thought he needed some blessings and protection from evil spirits and so she brought a picture of the Pope, dressed in his robes and wearing a big cross. She had it hung in the living room. She wanted to hang it over the family bed where Jesus slept with his parents but neither Jose' nor Maria wanted the Pope hanging out in their bedroom! To pacify granny, they consented to the living room.

Strangely, from then on, every time Jesus was carried into the living room and was in sight of the picture, he cried and cried, no matter who held him. He still cried more in grandma's arms, especially when she would spin the cross over his head in an attempt to pacify him.

It wasn't until he could crawl and point that he succeeded in communicating to everyone that he found crosses very disturbing and they were the source of his suffering. This was a great relief to Jose' and Maria, who immediately took down the Pope's picture and returned it to Grandma. Grandma was ambivalent about the discovery. On the one hand, it was good to know why he cried and that now she could go back to her original perfume and diet and not take his distress personally. She sorely missed her cabbage and garlic! On the other hand, she feared for his soul and could not understand why the symbol of Jesus' suffering and death would make him cry.

This unusual behavior, however, persisted throughout his childhood. It became more manageable for him once he began to speak and he could explain to those he encountered that he found the commemoration of nailing a man on a cross a rather strange and heartless thing to do and if they really wanted to continue to wear such a 'reminder' of another's pain and suffering, could they please tuck it under their shirts? This, they always did as he expressed himself in such an effective manner they felt compelled to comply. Oftentimes they looked at him strangely and remarked that his concern and his feelings made more sense than their own thoughtless, unquestioning and selfish religious and/or fashion statement.

Even Grandma, who had suffered severe blows to her self-esteem, loved him so much that when he visited, all crosses and crucifixes and pictures of saints were removed from view. It wasn't long before they were removed permanently, and strangely, even Grandma began to feel better, the unexplained stiffness in her fingers, arms and legs suddenly gone. A miraculous healing? Perhaps.

Grandpa also loved Jesus dearly and grew more and more convinced that he was called Jesus because he WAS Jesus; the one and only Jesus. How did he come to this conclusion? Mostly because he still couldn't stand the idea that Jose' was Jesus' real father and that Jose' had slept with his sweet, pure, perfect and virginal Maria. He decided and fully convinced himself, as people are prone to do, that Maria was impregnated by the Holy Spirit and was still a virgin. Jesus was, therefore, immaculately conceived now as it happened then. This did not seem at all far-fetched to him and he spoke openly and convincingly to others that this was obviously the case.

What he called the Immaculate Conception, Jose' and Maria knew to be the Immaculate Deception. Nothing new here, but what could they do but love the old guy anyway.

Jesus really loved animals. He was raised in a manger, more or less, and surrounded by animals. He crawled under cows and goats and wandered with chickens, fully integrating himself as a four-legged animal. The animals loved him too. Never once was he ever in danger, never once did a cow even come close to stepping on him, and never once was any animal unaware of his presence. When he became a two-legged animal, he played catch-the-cow's-tail, running back and forth giggling ecstatically as the cow watched him and swished her tail back and forth as Jesus tried to catch it. When he did, he never pulled it or caused his playmate any distress.

He learned to milk the cows and went on egg hunts; he went hiking in the desert with Jose' and Maria, watched and learned from the wild animals without intruding on their lives and their freedom.

No, he never miraculously played with a rattlesnake or a scorpion. He did find tarantulas fascinating and often had one or more crawling on him.

He often returned with hurt animals, ravens with hurt wings, hawks, various rodents, and set up his own animal hospital in a corner of the barn. It wasn't unusual to see Dr. Jesus performing 'miracles' surrounded by a gallery composed of curious cows, goats, even a desert tortoise or two. Perhaps the spirit of St. Francis was there too, but no one thought of that.

Jesus also loved to ride with Chika and the other bikers out into the desert and became good friends with his parent's friends' children. He was good natured and even the most hotheaded, hyper kids respected his love of all living things and learned from him to never hurt others, no matter what kinds of bodies they walked around in.

Did Jesus exhibit signs of future, miraculous behavior? Did his childhood foretell of greatness and saintliness? Was he different than all other children and destined for greatness like Tiger Woods or Michael Jackson?

He was bright, kind, curious and a lover of life.

Miraculous?

Definitely.

Chapter 7: Coming of Age

Jesus grew to be a very good looking young man, quiet and a little shy. He minded his own business and respected pretty much everyone. At school he avoided getting involved with any particular clique and shunned the local Hispanic gang entirely. For some reason, perhaps his quiet congeniality and lack of judgment, he was neither recruited nor bothered by the gang members. He liked everyone, stood beside the weak, disabled and disenfranchised, did his thing and smiled a lot. Everyone seemed to like him as well.

Considering the conservative, economically depressed place he lived, he was into some weird stuff. He kept up on environmental concerns and rode his bike as much as possible. He didn't drive a car. He was a vegetarian and an animal rights activist, a savior of stray dogs and cats and, like his mom and dad, ardent about the compassionate treatment of the cows at the dairy. He loved the cows so much that he wouldn't even use the automatic milking machines, filling the milk buckets with gentle hands on the cows' teats. He insisted that the baby calves get to drink their fill first before he would take the milk for selling. When Maria and Jose' would chide him about his extremism, he just laughed, looked his momma in the eye and said, "how would you have liked it if someone took me away from you when I was a baby, stuck two, cold, mechanical sucking mouths on your beautiful and full tits, and then sold your milk to the co-op?" Neither parent had much to say to counter Jesus' logic. They smiled, wondered what planet their son had come from, and gave silent thanks that he had come.

He liked to listen to interviews with Noam Chomsky on NPR.

Jesus wouldn't wear leather and had attempted to start an animal rights club at the high school. Some students, mostly girls, actually attended the first couple of meetings but soon dropped out when they felt they couldn't buy or wear leather shoes, belts or jackets. Jesus encouraged them to stay, even with their leather goods, but soon was left as the club's sole member. The club ceased to exist and Jesus did volunteer work at the no-kill animal shelter and donated half his allowance to the Best Friends Animal Shelter in Utah, a place he always wanted to visit. He also gave to other groups and liked collecting animal conservation stamps and return address stickers.

He wasn't totally weird. He liked to run, play ball and keep in shape. He was in such good shape that the girls, especially the older ones, loved looking at him. Although he was reticent about getting involved with any of the girls at school, he was aware of their attentions and enjoyed being the object of their amorous intentions. He did like to flirt and was a very good conversationalist, his most attractive trait being his eagerness to listen and learn.

He was seventeen and a senior at Barstow High when he first met Maria Magdalena Rodriquez. They didn't meet at school, because Maria was twenty-two and had already graduated. They met at the music store in the half deserted Barstow Mall. Jesus was buying some new strings for his guitar and Maria had just come from the backroom, where she was giving a drum lesson. Maria was really into percussion; a woman of perpetual rhythm. She was a very popular teacher.

Jesus could feel her energy as she walked behind him toward the front door. He looked up from the counter where his new strings lay and saw her reflection in the mirror behind the cash register. He was stunned! It was as if Maria, by her very being, had pounded out her rhythm on Jesus' chest, penetrating his heart for all eternity.

Jesus had never seen anything so beautiful and powerful and desirable ever before in his rather short life. She had dark skin and hair blue black like a raven. Her hair tumbled loose and free and wild over her shoulders. Her eyes were big, dark and doe-like and, to his delight, they turned toward him coyly and intently as she walked by, seeing him watching her in the mirror and enjoying it. Her lips were full and open and, it seemed to Jesus, hungry. *"Hungry for everything,"* Jesus thought. Jesus, lover of animals, had just seen the most exquisite and wildest of animals and wanted nothing else but to go on safari!

Maria was dressed all in tight fitting blue denim. Her jeans were tight around her hips and butt, narrowing as they descended past her knees, flaring out over her boots. She wore a tight, light, blue T-shirt molded over mounds of joy that rose and fell with the combined rhythm of her gait and her breath. Her open jean jacket completed the look of radical, revolutionary independence. On the collar of the jacket was pinned a button with PETA written on it.

The arrow of love and recognition pierced Jesus' heart. He was smitten. He would never be the same. Where had she come from? How had he never seen her before?

Maria Magdalena swayed and strode out the door of the music store and headed for the mall exit.

Jesus quickly paid for his guitar strings, shoved them into his jean jacket, and rushed after her. He caught up with her just outside, in front of the mall. Maria was leaning over, untying a leash from the bike rack near where Jesus' bike and another bike were locked. He stopped behind her and admired the view. On the other end of the leash was a brown and white, floppy-eared Bassett hound with a rather sardonic and droopy countenance. The dog was looking intently at Jesus and, to his amazement, winked and smiled at him. It seemed like a smile but, having never seen a dog smile, Jesus couldn't be sure. He had no doubt about the wink.

"Stop salivating and come over here." Maria said.

Jesus looked again at the dog, who was slobbering as Bassett hounds do.

"You," she said, "not Paul here. You're the one drooling behind me."

Jesus, shocked, discovered that he was the one salivating and Maria was talking to him. He quickly closed his mouth and joined her and Paul, realizing that was the dog's name.

They stood before each other and looked into each other's eyes. For Jesus, when he looked into Maria's eyes, he saw himself at Home inside of her, and he knew she saw and felt the same. It was as if they had known each other forever and seeing each other for the first time simultaneously. Time stood still; they shared eternity in that moment.

Maria smiled and Jesus melted.

"I'm Jesus," he told her.

"Yes, I know who you are. I'm Maria Magdalena Rodriquez," she replied in a voice full of song.

Maria turned and bent over to let Paul off his leash. She put the leash into her saddle bag and unlocked her bike, snapping the cable lock onto the frame. She pulled her bike off the rack, threw her leg over and straddled the seat.

Jesus wanted to be that bicycle seat.

"Come on. Unlock your bike and ride with me. This is your bike, isn't it?

Jesus keyed in his combination, unlocked the cable and wrapped it under his seat. He stepped on the pedal, pushed off and pulled up next to Maria. They rode off down Main Street. Paul, tongue hanging out, ran frantically on his short legs to keep up. His tail wagged happily, however, and he looked lovingly at Maria's new companion.

"Shouldn't we ride slower so Paul doesn't have to run so hard?" Jesus asked.

"Yes, we should," Maria replied, smiling, knowing Jesus was the kind of man to ask just such a question.

Slowing, she turned to Paul and winked.

"You set the pace, Jesus, and I'll tell you where to go."

"I'm happy to go anywhere you want," thought Jesus as they slowed their pedaling to accommodate Paul's short legs. Maria directed their journey until they arrived at the Sunrise Mobile Home Park off Windy Pass Road, not far from where Jesus' grandparents lived. Barstow is a small town and he again wondered why he had never seen Maria before.

"I'm a bit older than you and have been traveling for a few years," Maria responded to his thoughts. I left Barstow five years ago. I've been in Los Angeles doing some music gigs and then spent some time in Utah, doing conservation work at Capital Reef Park and also volunteering at the Best Friends Animal Shelter. That's where I fell in with Paul. He was the one who told me about you and that's why I came back here."

"Let's go inside," she said as she led him under the carport roof of trailer number 52, a single wide whose small surrounding space was planted with pomegranate bushes and a fig tree. "It's my theory that Eve ate a pomegranate way back when in the Garden. I don't think apples grew in that climate-too warm-and besides, pomegranates are

52

sinfully delicious and always make me horny. How about you, do they affect you that way?"

Jesus followed her into her home, excitedly curious about this gorgeous woman who talks to dogs and expresses theories about the role of different fruits in the Bible. Paul trotted up the wooden ramp next to the steps Maria had installed for him. Because he was vertically challenged, the steps dug into his belly. Paul hated steps, considering them a design flaw. He was a staunch supporter of the Disability Law that gave him greater access to human dwellings.

Maria offered him a seat on the flower-print sofa, then went into the little kitchen, opened the frig and took out a pitcher. She poured two glasses of a deep, rich, maroon colored liquid, gave one to her guest, sat down next to him and put her feet up on the glass topped, rattan coffee table, carefully placing them between the candle holders and books.

"Pomegranate juice and hibiscus flower tea," she said as she took a long, slow delicious drink.

Jesus followed suit, closing his eyes in pleasure as the cool, red, sweet-tart liquid filled his consciousness. In his mind the image of a lovely pool and a cool drink flashed before him. He began to feel he was in the Garden. There was certainly no place he would rather be!

Maria's home was small, cozy, colorful and sweet smelling. The walls were painted a light, sage green with terra cotta colored trim, perfectly suited to the desert

53

climate. There were potted plants, hanging plants, and a couple of over-stuffed, real wood bookcases.

"I'll explore her books later," he mused. *"You can really tell where someone is coming from by their library."*

The windows were draped with hand-dyed, multicolored, diaphanous cloth and pastel paintings of flowers and fruit hung on the walls. Next to the couch where they were sitting, Paul was recuperating from his run on his brown, corduroy covered doggy bed, his blood-shot, droopy eyes fixed on Jesus.

With his eyes also fixed on Paul, Jesus asked Maria, "So, Paul and you are best friends and he convinced you to come back here to Barstow? How exactly did he do that?"

"He told me it was time. He told me he had to be here to meet with and talk to you; he was sent here by, and I quote, "the Guy by the pool who had a marguerita with you."

Jesus' memory was stirred, and a bit shaken. Paul cocked his head as if he was looking for a sign of recognition.

"And how did he communicate this very specific message to you?"

"He spoke in my head. He also said it might take you a while to loosen your resistance to his entering your head as 'guys tend to be tighter and righter than gals'. That's just how he put it and it seems he's quite right. 'You can't limit the Possibilities of Consciousness' was another of his

54

simple, yet profound dictums. Paul's really quite a bright fellow and a fascinating conversationalist."

"Well," Jesus said somewhat skeptically while addressing Paul with a smile, "I look forward to long hours of conversation with you."

Paul sneezed and shook his head, spraying Jesus with drool. He put his head down and closed his eyes as if he was dismissing a foolish child.

"Let's you and I go to the drive-in tonight," Maria suggested.

"I don't have a car and I didn't see one in your carport either."

"No, I don't have a car. We can take our bikes, a blanket, a lantern and a picnic dinner and park ourselves in the desert outside the drive-in area. We can pick up the sound track on an AM radio, or not. Some movies are more fun without sound. And that way we can be alone together."

"I'm in."

Paul sneezed again and then growled quietly.

"He doesn't want to go," Maria told Jesus.

They spent the rest of the afternoon pleasantly talking about things that interested them: Music, animal rights, karma, the over abundance of aerial plastic bags flying through the desert. They prepared some cold, vegetarian salads to take with them. Jesus especially wanted to bring some more of the pomegranate-hibiscus tea combo. Time passed quickly and without notice until the sun sank low and the day darkened. They climbed on top of the mobile home and watched the desert sunset side by side, hand in hand, Being in silence in an awesome world.

After dark, they climbed down, and Jesus called his dad on his cell phone, gave him the short version of his meeting with Maria, and said he would be staying in town that night. Maria and Jesus then gathered up their stuff and left for their outdoor dinner. Paul lay asleep in his bed, snoring like an old man with asthma. As they walked out, Paul lifted his head and breathed deep with satisfaction, wagging his tail joyfully. *"At last, I am with him."*

Maria and Jesus eagerly hopped on their bikes and rode north across the bridge over the rail yards, past the stately old Harvey House and across the ever dry Mojave River. They continued on Old Highway 58 until they reached the drive-in movie and found a place to put out their blanket and the dinner picnic they packed. Maria pulled out four candles in hurricane lamps, lit them and placed one in each corner, one at each direction. They sat silently across from each other, eating and sharing their food, savoring the flavors, savoring each other's company. The movie came on and they paid no attention, watching instead the moon and stars as they rotated in the heavens.

They too rotated with the heavens, moving closer and closer together, two heavenly bodies that had been orbiting through life towards this moment of celestial conjunction. They lay close to each other, sharing their warmth. Their lips met and their eyes swam in the dark, liquid spaces of the other. They had found each other. They were in Love together. They were in Life together. They made out and touched each other for hours and Maria, older and with experience Jesus lacked, taught him about herself, taught him how to explore and discover her. Jesus' gentle and strong hands traveled eagerly and joyously over her exotic landscape. They took their time, neither wanting to finish such a good story anytime soon. Just before midnight, they packed up their things and rode back to Maria's where they spent the first of many nights together.

The next day, the two of them, together with Paul, rode out to meet Jose' and Maria. Jesus' parents fell in love with Maria instantly and Jose' was full of pride in his son and his beautiful woman. Before long, Jesus packed up his things and his guitar and moved in with Maria.

Chapter 8: Paul's Story

"You're the one my Father sent to bring me up to speed on my life's work?" Jesus asked Paul with some bemused astonishment.

"You have a problem with that? You think you're too good to have a dog fill you in on what you need to know? Are you going to be like everyone else in this world and let assumption overrule possibility. Your Dad would not be pleased."

"Actually," Jesus smiled, "I like the idea of learning from you. I find dogs to be quite straight forward in their expression. I'm just feeling a bit foolish and uncomfortable sitting here on all fours with you."

"Then sit in the chair kid. This conversation is mind to mind, heart to heart. It doesn't require eye contact or a level playing field. Sheesh, you take the "all creatures are equal" thing far too seriously. Equal but different. Well, dogs might be just a little bit superior and certainly more honest. No argument there I see."

"Sit!" Paul said. Jesus sat.

"Hmmm," thought Paul, *"That was cool."*

"Roll over," ordered Paul.

"Don't push your luck," Jesus said offhandedly.

"Sorry, can't blame a dog for trying. And if you don't mind, I'll just jump up on the couch with you in Your Name. Kind of a habit, doing things I'm not supposed to do in Your Name. Everyone does it. It's the problem I'm supposed to teach you about. It's been going on for two thousand years and I'm one of the ones who got it all started."

"Go on, I'm listening. What's your story?"

"Are you circumcised?"

"What's that?"

"Is your penis intact or are you genitally without your hood? Are you wearing a V-neck or a turtle neck? "

"No, I'm not circumcised and this is a strange man and dog conversation. Is this some kind of interspecies bonding? Are we going to have a pissing contest? Jerk off together? It's not my thing."

"No, no, none of the above, but when you come right down to it, we were all obsessed with penises. Back then, the chosen people had exposed 'heads' and the unchosen had their penises intact. We actually believed God sorted out His children by their cocks and that He liked us better if we practiced self-mutilation. Millions today still believe it so strongly that the majority of little boys, Jewish, chosen or not, are mutilated."

"Odd how we never questioned our beliefs, how we rarely question our beliefs. Such assumptive arrogance. Our

59

beliefs are unbelievable! Can you believe what we believe?"

Paul shook his ears in disbelief.

"I was known as the apostle for the uncircumcised. Peter the apostle for the circumcised. I changed my name from Saul (definitely a name for the circumcised), to Paul (kind of iffy). I chose my market for its greater potential. Besides, there wasn't much we could offer the already chosen, while the unchosen didn't like being the unchosen, so I chose the unchosen to sell them chosenness. Peter had a much harder sell but he was kind of a snob about the whole thing, always throwing out the 'don't throw pearls before swine' thing."

"The unchosen also really liked the idea that they could become chosen without having to have their penises painfully dehooded. It was a great selling point."

"One of my myriads of letters was published to that effect."

> *"On the contrary, when they saw that I had been entrusted with the gospel for the uncircumcised, just as Peter had been entrusted with the gospel for the circumcised (for he who worked through Peter making him an apostle to the circumcised also worked through me in sending me to the Gentiles), and when James and Cephas and John, who were acknowledged pillars, recognized the grace that had been given to me, they gave to Barnabas and me the right hand of fellowship, agreeing that we*

60

should go to the Gentiles and they to the
circumcised."

Epistle to the Galatians 2:7-9

Paul leaned over and began licking his member.

"I actually much prefer this uncircumcised, retractable model; feels less exposed. But I'm getting a head of myself."

Jesus rolled his eyes.

"I was a salesman in my father's business, and a damn good one, too! Dad was a tent maker and the market was booming. Camel trains were THE way to travel and Tarsus Tents made the best tents for the desert market. We had a full service line supplying arrow and dagger proof tents for Roman soldiers, business tents for traveling traders and salesmen, luxury tents for wealthy sheiks and sultans, even one-room, cave-like tents for wandering, mystical hermits and other anti-socialites. I believe even John the Baptist carried a Tarsus Tent!"

"We had offices (yes, business tents) at all the best watering holes and I traveled constantly keeping our clients supplied, doing market research and creating new designs based on the ever changing needs of the economy. I knew our clientele and I was unbiased, treating all our diverse customers with equal respect."

"There were those who criticized my methods, claiming I had no discrimination and no true loyalties. They said I was an opportunist. They were right. I didn't play favorites; rather I favored everyone who could play, er...pay. Everyone liked to travel and we were in the RV business at the juncture of time when BC (backwards counting) changed to AD (accounting goes direct)."

"I was a good old boy. I was in love with attention and power. I was, well, narcissistic just like everyone else. Well, maybe a little more than everyone else."

"I was well positioned with both the Jewish community and the Romans and was a well respected man about town, providing top quality shelter for rolling stones from every walk of life. And I had clout in the temple, too. Money and power went hand in hand back in those days and hasn't changed much since."

Paul jumped down from the couch and trotted over to his water bowl. He lapped, shook his head and flapped his ears like a helicopter, clearing his head. He jumped back onto the couch, repositioned himself next to Jesus and continued his narrative.

"Then you came along, performing miracles, kicking the money changers out of the temple, telling everyone that money wasn't everything. Oy, you were pretty convincing and oh so charismatic. I never met you in person but I didn't like what you had set in motion. I was a conservative and your agenda was pretty liberal, you being so tolerant of women, prostitutes, sinners and the like. When you were disposed of, the conservative faction thought you and your ideas would go away, but it turned out to be only the beginning of a movement that has picked up speed and compounded falsehood and fantasy, exploitation, intolerance and violence for over two thousand years!"

Jesus shifted nervously on the couch, not liking what he was hearing.

"Oh it wasn't your fault," said Paul, picking up on Jesus' concern, "unless you can be blamed for being so attractive and convincing. You only wanted to help people, and you did. That's why you were crucified. Powerful and defensive people do what they can to remove those they perceive as threatening."

"It was actually my fault and the fault of those who followed me, right up to the present moment. We were the ones who fashioned and marketed Christianity, branded it, competed with other religious products. We created the cult of Jesus, selling you as the Christ, the savior; selling ourselves as the priests, intermediaries and interpreters of your life. You had left. We took advantage of that, resurrecting you and having visions when needed. In short, we set you up. You were gone and we used you. You couldn't have known."

"At first I was recruited by the conservatives to put an end to the whole movement by persecuting, imprisoning and killing your followers. We figured well-placed and persistent intimidation would suffice. We were wrong. We had martyred you, and persecuting your followers only gave them more strength and determination. We of all people, gaining strength throughout our history from persecution, should have known better."

"I was on the way to Damascus with a big persecution coming up when I realized I couldn't win and decided 'if you can't beat them, join them.' I was becoming the unpopular hit man and I didn't like it. I didn't even like the guys I was working for."

"It was time to fall off a horse and remount in a different direction. I hit the ground pretty hard, saw a bright light and knocked something loose in my head. I was shook up, temporarily lost my sight and, as history has recorded, heard your voice asking me why I was being such a hard-hearted bastard. Did you actually speak to me? I don't know. It could have been you speaking from a different dimension, or it could have been me talking to myself, telling me what I wanted to hear. How many 'visions' are spiritual visitations? How many are psychotic episodes? Schizophrenics hear voices and see things, charlatans pretend to experience supernatural episodes, and every televangelist tells everyone that God speaks directly to them!"

"What's important to understand here isn't whether the vision was real but rather what I chose to do with it. In my experience, you just asked me why I was being such a bad ass and tormenting the friends you had left behind, you didn't tell me to start a cult and recruit members from across the tracks. You certainly didn't suggest I become the apostle for the people of the retractable dickheads!"

"So, I joined your team, added my zeal and convincing marketing experience and created a monster that is not only still reproducing, but serving as a model for the creation of other monsters."

Paul laid his head down sheepishly on Jesus' feet, closed
his eyes and with a sigh, spoke a deep, heartfelt, remorseful
"sorry."

Jesus put his hand on Paul's head and petted him gently,
first scratching one ear and then the other. Paul moaned
with doggy pleasure, marveling at love's simplicity,
knowing that a true spiritual experience can simply be an
ear lovingly scratched.

"Thank you, God," Paul prayed, *"for giving me this chance
at redemption and for giving me the body of a dog!"*

Jesus smiled and said, "apology accepted. I understand
your part and acknowledge your contribution to what
humans have done in the name of religion since those in
'power' invented it. It was done before I came the first time
and before you played your part. I'm sure others followed
to create the dangerous situation in which we now find
ourselves. What can you tell me of that and where do we go
from here?"

Paul, having confessed and feeling as light as a Bassett
Hound can feel, continued to bring Jesus up to date on the
happenings of the last two thousand years.

Chapter 9: How It All Got Screwed Up: Religion's Legacy

Paul continued barking about The Problem.

"It seems to be a human trait to spiritualize perversions and fears, and then defend them with great fervor. God has been made into a convenience, a scapegoat, a concocted, Supreme Justification. Afraid of women and too weak to embrace sexuality? God tells you to burn them. Afraid of Gays and Lesbians? God tells you to beat them up and condemn them to hell. Can't stand Jews? God tells you they were Christ killers and they should be exterminated. Christian and hateful of Muslims? The children of Cain can never be redeemed; do away with them God tells you. Muslim and hateful of Christians? God guarantees Paradise if you blow them up. Do you like sex with young girls? God reveals to you that it's your sacred duty to marry as many as you can convince you are divinely led. Your Hindu God says it's good to kill Muslims, your Muslim God says it's good to kill Hindus, Christians and Jews, your Jewish God says its good to kill Muslims, your Christian God used to say its good to kill Jews but not now as your book hints that the Jews and the rebuilding of the Jewish temple are needed to bring Christ back. Afraid and/or scornful of women? Your Jewish, Christian, Muslim and Hindu God tells you that women are inferior, your property, yours to do with as you like.

Gods smods, These are not Gods. These are comic book villains."

"Religion became a comic book written by immoral authors dressed as priests and popes, emperors and scholars, who hired artists to illustrate their stories of fear and retribution and present them to the illiterate populace on the walls of churches, all the while engaged in the very activities they held up as forbidden and condemnatory."

"The artists, especially in the Renaissance, had a very hard time, much preferring to illustrate the amorous activities of the Greek Deities. Michelangelo, who never wanted to paint the ceiling of the Sistine Chapel and was coerced by the Pope (who thought himself to be Julius Caesar), even went so far as to add his own lewd touches as a retort to the sanctimonious sinners braying…er…praying below. In his panel where God is creating the Planets and the Stars, One of the celestial figure's flowing robes are placed so that he appears to be shining his Divine Moon down on those below. And Adam is certainly left holding the tree limb as Eve finds the fruit offered by the serpent more attractive than his own limp dick. Art history books seem to have overlooked these impertinent statements and artists mostly kept to the program, needing the wherewithal to eat, drink and have sex, straight and gay."

"Even the priests that were fanatical and unhealthy enough to resist all 'sin,' fared poorly. Savonarola zealously condemned the artists for their hedonistic work and initiated the "Bonfire of the Vanities," burning paintings by Botticelli and books and paintings by other heretical artists. He proclaimed God would end the world at the turn of the century (1500) because of all the sinners. He was partly right as the world did end… for him. The Pope had him fire roasted as a heretic, putting an end to his attempts at spoiling the fun!"

Paul looked up at Jesus and then put his head down, feeling ashamed.

"There were and are confusing aspects to all this in that those who were 'sinless' or pretended to be, claimed that you would punish the sinners with your wrath, sending them to hell on the Judgment Day, while the sinners believed they were saved from hell because they had accepted you into their hearts and were thus forgiven. The priests duly profited from this confusion by assuring the sinners that they would be sinless if they paid them a fee. These arbiters of divine behavior even went so far as to guarantee the heavenly release of the sinfully deceased for a few bucks more."

"Excuse me," Paul said, "I have to drink some more water and perhaps we could continue our conversation on a walk? This stuff gives me a headache!"

Paul jumped down from the couch, took another drink from his bowl and pushed through his dog door onto the porch. Jesus followed him out (through the human door). Paul trotted ahead, turned to Jesus and said, "heel boy."

Jesus laughed and caught up with his four legged friend.

"No offense meant," Paul grunted. "I've wanted to say that to a human for a long time."

"No offense taken. Humans have their hierarchies of species upside down anyway."

It was a fine afternoon and the sun was getting low in the western sky. Jesus and Paul walked in silence for a time, enjoying the quiet, the air and especially their companionship. They were old friends really and Paul, though he filtered Jesus' teachings through his own ego and made mistakes, loved him deeply and sincerely. He wondered why it seemed so much easier to love as a dog than as a human?

Paul broke the silence with two, low grunts.

"What was that?" asked Jesus.

"Fear and greed," Paul said again, this time in Jesus' head so he could understand.

"Fear and greed have been and still are major motivators for screwing up everything you came to model."

"Fear of what?" Jesus wondered out loud.

"Fear of life, fear of death, fear of nature and fear of woman. It seems that these are all synonymous in the ego mind of men. This fear is the most integral thread of the Judeo-Christian Story, woven deeply into the Old Testament. One of the reasons you were killed was because you weren't afraid and that threatened the power structure. How could people who were not afraid be manipulated and controlled? So you were killed and the fear grew even stronger. You said the Truth shall set you free, that all

God's children are sacred, even the sinners, the women; you even said that to know heaven required the mind of a child! So you were killed so everyone would remember that the Truth will get you killed."

"Then you were set up as the sacrifice. You had to die because 'God' wanted you sacrificed so that those who believed in you could be saved, even if they still fucked up.""

"That makes sense, doesn't it," Paul said sarcastically.

"I don't understand any of it. I'm getting a headache now, too. So people believe my Father loved me so much that He arranged for me to meet a cruel and painful death so that my brothers and sisters could be saved? Saved from what? People are no different now than they were then, perhaps more violent, hateful, fearful, intolerant and unforgiving than ever. And I know my Father; He wouldn't do something so unloving and insane."

"Ah, but His children have been ready and willing to war and kill in His, and your, names. To make a long and miserable story short, the Judeo-Christian perspective and all the cults, whether culturally recognized or abhorred, have relegated nature and all the animals and plants inferior to humans, denying that any creature save man has a soul and denying them access to 'heaven,' wherever and whatever that might be. The general Jewish and Christian belief is that God gave man dominion over all other creatures; 'dominion' taken as permission to corral, kill, exploit and eat as many as possible. And since 'heaven' is our true home, and earth but a temporary test of 'faith,' what happens to her is of little consequence; we can do with her what we like. They think of the earth like they think of a woman, property to be bought, sold, maintained or raped as we like."

"Sex and sensuality became synonymous with the sinful temptations of a strange, concocted creature called the devil who supposedly first worked his evil on Eve, who then infected Adam, resulting in their expulsion from paradise. The story really didn't have anything to do with sex. It was actually about mental, egoistic delusion. God didn't want his newly created children to partake of the fruit of the tree of good and evil. There wasn't any good or evil, or rather, it was all good, but because with God all things must be possible, the mental state of duality is also possible. So Adam and Eve chose to 'eat' of the fruit of delusion and thus lost sight of the paradise they were still actually a part of. That delusion has become the normal state of God's children here on earth. The Garden is still here, but we have covered it up and destroyed it because we are busy fighting with each other about right and wrong, good and evil. We were never expelled by a wrathful God. We never even left. We just became totally preoccupied with unreal concepts and unrelenting and hideous attempts to remake creation in accordance with those concepts. The 'devil' is our own deluded self-concept, a concept so small and inconsequential, yet so insistent, clever, false and manipulative that it fills up our entire screen of consciousness, leaving no room, no space for the reality of Infinity. So clever is this false self that it has projected itself and its qualities outside, creating and recreating a creature we call the devil. It was first fashioned by early Christians as an adaptation of the Greek God Pan, a lusty satyr who loved to dance, drink, have sex and make merry, and the Egyptian God of troublemaking named Seth, sometimes Sethan. To recruit and control converts, the beliefs and practices of the 'pagans' had to be vilified, so this devil was fashioned from the pagan god and the activities of that god became 'sinful.' And because (in the story) Eve was the first to be seduced, woman became the personification of sin and temptation. Woman, who is the gateway to Life, was recast in league with the devil, the agent who would drag men into desire, sin and earthly pleasure, the one who seduced men away from God and into hell."

"This totally ridiculous, insane and horrific doctrine became translated into the murder of millions of women at the hands of Christian Inquisitors who judged anyone with a connection to nature, herbs, birth, death, overt or subtle sexuality, to be in league with the devil, judged a witch who had to be burned at the stake. They had to be killed lest they, like Eve, tempt the men into disobedience and sinfulness in the sight of their god. They had to be killed to continue Adam's legacy of wimpiness."

"Emperors, beginning with Constantine, the first 'Holy Roman Emperor," claimed they had seen you in their dreams and visions and that you had guaranteed them victory in battle if they fought in your name, under your banner. They did and they won; their divine connection became 'fact,' and again, those with military might had reestablished Divine Monarchy. Prior to the cult grown around your killing, rulers simply claimed themselves descendents of the gods but since we created the monopoly of the Son of God and the One True Way, they had to have your real or imagined endorsement."

"Of course this led to problems when more and more divinely chosen visionaries began competing with each other, and when One True Way crossed paths with Another True Way and the followers of gods that may or may not have even existed fought to the death with each other, killing everyone and everything that came near. Huge problems arose when All the Followers of All the Only True Ways All laid claim to the same Holy Lands. Together with the advent of military technology, the Holy lands became the Holey Lands, saturated with the blood of two thousand years of war."

"It's still going strong today and things are worse than ever, all because of me and the other so-called disseminators of 'Christianity."

"How so," asked Jesus, worry again in his voice.

"One of your followers was very pissed off at the Roman rulers responsible for your death. He was a zealous preacher of your divinity and he was shipped off to a prison island where he spent his old age. While he was there, he had visions of you where you instructed him to write down his 'revelations,' which included warnings of imminent disasters that would be rained down on all humanity who did not embrace your divinity. He said these disasters would occur very, very soon, followed by your second coming, and then the Lord would destroy all those deluded and controlled by the Beast."

"So far, this has not come to pass and 'very, very soon' has been stretched out 2000 years. It seems likely that these 'revelations' were the ranting of a crazy and angry old man, yet there are millions of 'Christians' today who still believe these things will happen. They believe so strongly that everything that happens in today's world is viewed as obvious signs of prophesy coming to pass. They believe so strongly and want this destruction of the 'unbelievers' to happen so bad, they just might do everything they can, in the name of God and Jesus, to make it happen. They even have the means to do it, the destruction that is."

"According to them, you're here too soon."

"I'm not here to fulfill anyone's prophesies." Jesus said. "I didn't have anything to do with all that shit."

"I know," replied Paul, "We set you up and it's been getting worse and worse."

"Wow," was all Jesus could say. "Let's go get some ice cream. Do you like ice cream?"

"Cool," said Paul, wagging his tail. "I really like chocolate but I've been told dogs shouldn't eat chocolate. Is that true?"

"I have heard that too, so no chocolate for you!"

"Damn!"

They trotted off together to get some dessert in the desert.

Chapter 10: The Group

Maria, Jesus and Paul became a family that spent all their time together. They did a lot of hiking, biking, and, as Jesus and Maria liked the same songs and played music together, began busking at parks and malls. There wasn't much of a music scene in the High Desert, nor were they paid much mind by passersby, but they loved playing together and picked up enough cash to cover their meager expenses. When a crowd did gather, Paul, a real ham (dogs could be hams), would dance around on his hind legs and wave to the crowd with his forepaws. He would howl in tune and make everyone laugh. Even in his dog body, he still knew how to work a crowd and always increased their take.

Their favorite place to sing was the Farmer's Market at Victor Valley College on Thursday mornings. Besides the gaiety of all the colorful fruits and vegetables and the camaraderie of the vendors, the market was a gathering place of many with alternative ideas and lifestyles. Ecologically minded people manned booths dedicated to saving the desert flora and fauna from the perpetual onslaught of all-terrain vehicles, Native Americans sold pipes, turquoise, sage smudge sticks, and spoke to those who would listen about their powwows and the interconnectedness of All Our Relations, and Jesus and Maria sang songs of Peace.

It wasn't long before they became a magnetic core, attracting other like-minded people and musicians and the Thursday morning market became a regular celebration of cultural diversity and peace. Two of the regulars, Luke and Marcus, became so much a part of the group that they too moved in with Maria, Jesus and Paul and the four of them began to take themselves seriously as musicians and songwriters.

Luke, whose real name was Lucinda, played base guitar. Her preference had always been for short hair and men's clothes and had been called Luke since she was a child. Sexually, she preferred women but her constant companion and best friend was a gay guy named Marcus who played the fiddle. Marcus wrote gospel songs and, together with Luke, they were working on a CD called "The Gospel According to Marcus." They argued a lot and Jesus told Luke she should play backup on Marcus' Gospel and Luke should record her own Gospel album with Marcus' backup.

Maria's trailer became a meeting place for the musical and peace-minded of the high desert. Over time, young, middle-aged and old found their way there every weekend to celebrate with song, dance and discussions about the state of the world, and what they could together do to make their place and their lives healthier and happier. Paul was happier than he had ever been in any of his lives and went from person to person to get scratched, petted and rubbed. He spent hours lying on his back while his fan club took turns rubbing his belly. The muscles of his rear, right leg were getting stronger and stronger from his involuntary scratch reflex.

The rest of the week, Jesus, Maria, Marcus and Luke took their musical work very seriously, writing and arranging new songs, rehearsing and rearranging old songs, developing a repertoire to take on the road that clearly represented who they were and what they felt was essential to say. They named their band Sibling Revelry to celebrate their brother and sisterhood and to counter a world bent on genocide. They began playing everywhere they could. They played outside the music store in the Vons shopping center on Bear Valley Road, they played at the market, they played at Barstow Community College, they played at Victor Valley College, and they played at restaurants and a club called Pappi's and Harriets over by Joshua Tree.

One day, they were playing in a Victorville shopping center, outside the theater complex, where "The Passion of the Christ" was playing. They went inside...

Chapter 11: Backlash

Mal (short for Malibu) Gypsome was working up a sweat on his Stairmaster, keeping his muscular, handsome and, in his opinion, Aryan body in powerful shape. He prided himself on his heritage and his attractiveness, never doubting that he knew exactly what women wanted. Knowing that, he did everything he could to remain in demand.

Mal lived luxuriously in his Malibu home, making a very good living doing various promotions and subsidizing various productions both legitimate and shady. He was well connected and well respected around town.

He was really working hard, full on into his aerobic routine when a breaking story on his new, gigantic, HDTV caught his attention. He slowed his virtual climb to a stop and stared open-mouthed at the screen! Christy Current, a young, attractive, blond reporter on the morning news, was sitting before a headline that read "Jesus Stands Up For Jesus," and was talking excitedly, her pale cheeks and pale chest flushed with excitement.

"A young, and I must say, very handsome man has made the news in this small town of Victorville in the Southern California desert causing quite a stir when he interrupted the showing of The Passion of the Christ in the local movie theater. We go now to Christy Timely who is at the scene with more.

The camera jumped to another young, attractive, blond reporter, possibly a clone, twin or close relative of the anchorwoman who introduced her. She was standing in the rear of the theater where hundreds of people in the audience were on their feet, filling the isles chanting "No More Violence, Jesus has suffered enough, No more violence, Jesus has suffered enough," over and over, led by a serious and spirited Hispanic youth.

"Yes Christy," Christy said with the voice of someone who was on-the-scene in a timely manner, "just about an hour ago, during the scene in the movie where Jesus was being brutally beaten by the Roman soldiers in Jerusalem, while the Jews watched gleefully and Satan glowered in the form of a woman with maggots coming out of her nose, this young man, whose name I have been told is actually Jesus Christo and a member of a music group called Sibling Revelry who were busking earlier in front of the theater, jumped onto the stage, tears in his eyes crying 'enough, enough, I cannot take anymore pain! How many times must Jesus be crucified?!' He then became very angry, yelling at all the people in the theater, 'Why are you here? Why are you so enthralled with watching the suffering of others? What is wrong with you that you take pleasure in others' pain? Can you possibly believe that you love Jesus and that he can feel any love from someone who crucifies him over and over and over again!'?"

"At that point, all the people in the theater stood up and began chanting what you are hearing right now, with the young Jesus in the lead."

Just then, on the stage, Jesus held up his hand and the crowd became silent, watching, waiting and listening.

Jesus began, speaking quietly, tears still in his eyes. "I can forgive you, for you do not know what you are doing. And you have been misled for centuries by others who do know what they are doing and do not care. The man who made this movie is using Jesus' suffering to make millions of dollars! And you are supporting him; you are supporting the continual crucifixion of he who truly loves you. He who made this movie, you who watch this movie, and everyone who reenacts and supports the crucifixion betrays Jesus again and again. Now you know. Now you must go and never support acts like this again for now you do know what you do. Enough!"

Christy Timely continued: "Well, there you have it. A brave young man with a heart of gold is changing the hearts and actions of the people here in the Inland Empire. Back to you Christy for a Current traffic update in the LA area." She giggled and rolled her eyes at her cleverness.

Mal was in shock! He couldn't believe what he just saw and what he knew millions of other people just saw on the news. The built-in blood pressure measuring device on his Stairmaster was beeping to him that he was experiencing severe hyper-tension and the sexy, computer voice was telling him to breathe deep and breathe slow. He paid no attention, picked up his cell phone and dialed a number on a secure line. "Come on, assholes," he muttered, "pick up the phone. Come on, come on, shit!"

A recording came on. "You have reached the Anti-Semitic Secret Society for the Preservation and Continuance of the Suffering of Jesus, please leave a message after the moan. Oooh, ooh, God it hurts, beep."

"Did you see the news? Get the boys together as soon as possible, I'll be at the office in an hour." Mal flipped his phone closed, took a quick shower, dressed, pocketed his flask and drove off in a hurry.

Chapter 12: The Campaign for Non-violent Accountability

Jesus left the theater in Victorville through the rear door and met with his compadres as planned. Maria, Luke and Marcus had joined the theater audience anonymously helping to get the energy and the chanting going. They were all hyped at the response and ecstatic about the unexpected news coverage. Paul, who had to wait outside, was also yipping and jumping, sharing his friends' joy and piecing together what happened from their conversations.

"Let's go back to our place and talk about what to do next," Jesus suggested.

They jumped into Luke's small car and sped off towards Barstow, Maria's head out the front window, enjoying the wind blowing through her hair, Paul's head held high out the rear window, ears flapping in the wind.

Back at their trailer, they gathered in the living room, draping themselves over the ragtag furniture and sitting cross-legged on the carpet. Paul curled up in his doggy bed and began snoring. Everyone else began talking all at once.

"Slow down," Jesus said in his quiet, yet unassailable voice. "We have to be focused and keep our goals in mind. We are here to counter the awful and destructive effects of the Cult of Jesus created from the pain of some very unfortunate events and decisions made two thousand years ago. Paul understands what happened better than any of us, as Jesus was already tortured and he played a big part in building the cult now known as Christianity."

Paul, still sleeping, began whimpering between snores, as though Jesus' words were conjuring up bad dreams. He rolled over suddenly, howled and woke himself up. He looked up at Jesus with that sorrowful and sorry look only Bassett Hounds can bear, then sneezed as if he was ridding himself of something disgusting.

Jesus continued. "Humans are cultural beings. That means we are cult crazy and we can very easily end up creating a whole new cult. I can just see it in the headlines: 'Jesus returns to set the course of Christianity in a new direction. Thousands pay him homage and clamor for the creation of The New Church of the Second Coming.' It's likely that all we'll really accomplish, even if we are careful, is to create more factions, inspiring more unscrupulous people to exploit the human need to belong."

"Our purpose is to debunk the myth that there was or ever will be a savior. Our purpose is to end the insanity that the suffering and killing of one man, no matter who he is, has or ever will excuse the lack of compassion of another."

Jesus, failing to comprehend how this idea could be born and take such firm root in the world's consciousness, sneezed and shook his head, as if in answer to Paul's excretory sneeze sounded a moment before.

Marcus asked, "Aren't we being Divinely guided? I mean, what we are doing feels so right, how can we not succeed?"

"No!" Jesus said as he looked at him and then around to the others. "NO!"

Again, Paul sneezed.

"We are Divinely created, Divinely inspired and Divinely free to totally fuck things up, over and over and over. Every cult and every nut case throughout history was 'Divinely guided,' from Constantine to Hitler. We don't want power and we don't want followers. We don't want to create or become a group separate or better than anyone else. We want to tell the Truth. We want to Be the Truth that we are and we want everyone to Be the Truth that they are, because everything, animate and inanimate is already created in God's Image. Everything IS God's Image. We are Divine. We don't need to be Divinely inspired."

"And mostly, we want everyone to rely on themselves and each other, finding their compassion and discovering that they ALL belong, not only to this group or that group, this country or that country, this race or that race, this culture or that culture, this religion or that religion, but to LIFE and LOVE Itself."

"So what's next?" Luke asked.

"We follow the advice of Tina Turner."

"Tina who?"

"Tina Turner, the brilliant, beautiful and sexy singer with the most perfect legs. My mom and dad turned me on to her. She was in a movie with Mel Gibson, the guy who produced and directed "The Passion." The movie was "Mad Max: Return to Thunderdome. It was one of those post-apocalypse movies this catastrophe prone culture loves so much and Mel, as always, plays the role of the reluctant, male hero, the same role that Jesus was cast in (concrete) two millennia ago."

"So what's Tina Turner's advice?" they all eagerly wanted to know.

"'We don't need another Hero!' It's a line in one of her songs."

Jesus sat silent, goading his friends to keep asking.

"Well," they said, getting annoyed, "How does that translate into what we need to do?"

"We need to go on doing what we're doing, playing our music, writing and singing songs of peace, songs of love for our planet and for each other, songs that express the name of our band, reveling in brotherly/sisterly love. We have to transform the 'Passion of Christ' the needless suffering imposed on one man, into the 'Compassion for Christ,' the care in the hearts of all people for all Creation. The Christ isn't one man, the Christ is the name for God's Son and God's Son IS the whole Creation. We are ALL the Christ. Then we will all know we must stop the unnecessary killing."

"So," Jesus continued, "next Sunday we play in Ontario, then at the fair in Riverside and on towards LA."

"Maria, Luke and Marcus, you guys used to play in LA, didn't you?"

"We played at a cute and cozy little venue for folk singers called McCabe's. It's a music store in Santa Monica with a theater in the back," Marcus answered.

"Can you book us there?"

Luke smiled. "Done."

Chapter 13: Epiphany

Mal was anxious about all the attention the Hispanic Jesus and his band was receiving and was really pissed off that Jesus encouraged people to boycott functions that included the crucifixion. It deeply irked him. He was psychologically invested in the belief that his own freedom to act depended on the suffering of Jesus, that Jesus went to his death to save him and others who believed in his sacrifice. He also had a deep hatred for the people, those Jews, whom he believed were responsible for the very act he was dependant on for his own salvation. Whenever he thought about these things and tried to figure them out, he got a migraine headache. It was easier to hate, easier to accept and maintain the status quo in regards to beliefs. Violence and suffering were also big business and he was a supporter of violent movies. This Jesus was bad mouthing violence; he was bad for business and he was pushing the idea, successfully, that he, Mal, along with every other Christian, was wrong about why what had happened happened! The pounding in his head jumped up another notch.

The question he struggled painfully with was how to stop him?

Every time the news covered the actions of this new age band of alien immigrants (or descendents thereof), Mal grew more morose, more obsessed, and more determined to take some kind of action himself. He had tried planting some of his men at the places Jesus appeared to draw the crowds back to the real message of Jesus, but it didn't work. None of his men were good looking enough and none even close to intelligent enough to counter the kid's charisma and logic. Mal knew that even he wasn't smart enough, or a good enough debater to go head to head with him. Mal was certainly handsome and virile enough (he preened a little at the thought of his good looks and his headache abated just a little), but he preferred to work behind the scenes. He was really a bit uncomfortable being out in the open or in the limelight. He was a sneaky guy, though this truth about him would be fiercely defended against and anyone who might even imply that he was a sneaky guy would find some unpleasant and unexpected surprise before too long. Sneaky indeed!

"How can I stop him? How can I stop him? How can I stop him?" It became a mantra, a throbbing question that pulsed in time with the throbbing pain in his head. He felt like he was going to go fucking crazy.

Then suddenly the pounding stopped. His mind became clear; suddenly he was in tune with who he was and what he must do. He realized, in that moment, that the fate and well-being of Christianity depended on him! He was the chosen one; he the very protector of the power and reputation of Jesus Himself! He remembered again why he had created the Secret Anti-Semitic Society for the Preservation and Continuance of the Suffering of Jesus.

"I," thought Mal, *"I alone must stop this guy. I alone have been divinely inspired and empowered to do the right thing. I am St. George who slays the dragon!"*

"Wow, that's a rush."

Mal just had to go and look at himself in the mirror, just had to see the chosen one, the hero. He stood tall and straight, straightened his hair and leaned closer.

"You're some kind of awesome, badass kind of guy!" he said to himself, wondering why he was talking so strangely. Then he leaned over even further and winked at himself. He had an incredible urge to kiss his own reflection but stopped with the passing thought that that was also strange…and someone might find out.

Satisfied with his revelation, and how he looked while having had a revelation, he began to map out how he would save traditional Christianity, keep Christ in Christmas, get rid of this HeyZeus guy and his message of accountability and, this was sheer genius, extend the culpability of the Jews!

Mal started to hop around the room in sheer glee. He felt like the Easter Bunny hopping around Jesus on the cross.

He picked up his phone and dialed a number.

"Prop Shop," a guy said as he answered Mal's call.

"This is Mal Gypsome. I need something made for an event I'm planning."

"Sure, Mal, shoot."

I need you to make me thirteen latex noses, each different, but each based on the shape and size of Adrien Brody, the Je…, er, the actor."

"Weird," thought the prop man, *"but this guy has always been a bit weird."*

"Sure," he replied. "I can have them for you in about two weeks."

"Perfect," Mal chirped, "send them to my home FedEx and bill my account." He could hardly contain himself over his own cleverness.

He hung up, slipped his phone into his pocket, pirouetted out the door, into the garage and drove off humming Zippity-do-da, Zippidy-ay until he remembered the song was written by Disney to celebrate the stories of Uncle Remus, a black man.

Chapter 14: The Agency

Judas was leaning back on his chair, feet on his cluttered desk, listening to his favorite Dylan song.

Booming out of his stereo issued the words of his absolutely favorite line that implied that Judas might have had God on his side.

Judas closed his eyes in bliss, ever amazed at the ingenuity and audacity of his favorite singer. Of course, he had taken an awful lot of crap his whole life because of his name and he still harbored a good bit of anger towards his parents, yet deep down he liked and felt quite connected to his name. His mother, bless her heart and her chicken soup, always insisted that one day he would understand why she named him Judas. He thought that Bob must also know why he was named Judas and that "God On His Side" was written especially for him.

Deeply believing in the innocence of his Biblical namesake, he had even named his small Hollywood actors' agency, Judas' Chariot, wanting only to be an advocate, never a betrayer. His mother had raised him to be a very honest and trustworthy young man.

"Judas is a good name and he was a good man," she would tell him. "He was framed. The Romans needed a fall guy. I know, trust me on this." Then she would give him a big hug, lead him to the table and say, "Eat, you are too skinny. Everyone in this country is either too skinny or too fat. No one remembers how to cook and nourish themselves. Oy!"

Judas always wondered how she could be so sure about the frame job, but she had a way of knowing things that was spooky and uncanny. He did trust her.

He leaned forward and hit the back button on the stereo to play his song again. *"Not many songs about a guy named Judas,"* he mused, *"unless you count Lennon's 'Hey Jude,'"* another song he liked and found encouraging. He had no doubt that both Lennon and Dylan were Prophets.

Things were very slow for his business as most of the work, both for agents and producers, was monopolized by people with connections to the big studios. Judas, though sociable and affable, was not very aggressive. He actually preferred to be left alone and only did as much recruiting of clients as he needed to stay afloat. He had some good actors as clients and some friends at the studios who called him regularly.

He had just gotten up to grab his guitar and his Bob Dylan Songbook when he heard a car screech to a halt in the handicapped parking space in front of his office. As he looked out his window, he saw a slick looking guy in an expensive car slip a handicapped marker over the stem of his rearview mirror. As Mal got out of his car, Judas noticed two things about him; he certainly wasn't handicapped, and he had a crazed look in his eyes.

Judas went back behind his desk, sat down, folded his hands on the desk, waited and wondered who this guy was and what he wanted.

Mal opened the door, strode in purposefully and sat down in the chair opposite Judas. He sat there and looked around the office as though he was taking inventory. Actually, he was taking inventory. Then he looked at Judas with a knowing, smug, feeling sorry for this guy, look.

Judas, always polite, asked, "Can I help you?"

"Actually," Mal smirked, "I'm here to help you." He looked around again, nodding his head and tisking as though he was trying to help Judas intuit something important.

After a moment's silent reflection, Judas asked, "OK, how can you help me?"

Chuckling to himself and acting like a man who knew something no one else knew, Mal leaned forward and said importantly and condescendingly, "I have something I want you to do. I have a job for you and (looking around a third time) it looks like you need the work." Mal was getting a little perturbed by Judas' lack of excitement. *"This Judas guy is Jewish,"* he thought. *"He's supposed to be greedy."*

"Let's take a step back," Judas said quietly. "My name is Judas. I am an actor's agent. Who do I have the pleasure of speaking to?" Judas didn't like the man sitting smugly across from him, but he could use the work. As he asked Mal to introduce himself, he saw both surprise and irritation on his guest's face and Judas realized he was supposed to have recognized him.

Mal, offended, pulled in his anger with internal promises of future reprisals.

"My name is Mal Gypsome. I am a television and movie producer. I am currently working with William Pontius, celebrity reality show moderator, in the production of a new, weekly, educational television series."

"What's the show about?" asked Judas

Mal fidgeted a little and looked down momentarily. He didn't like Judas' calmness and he hated that this pissy little Jew didn't recognize him as a mover and shaker. His plan required that this particular agent do his bidding, so he centered himself and continued.

"It's an educational show, a discussion forum focusing on important and relative current events as regards politics, entertainment and theology."

Judas leaned forward, becoming more curious. "What's it called and why have you come to my agency?"

Mal winced a little, concerned that this guy might not go for his proposal. "It's called "Exposed". It pits a panel of authorities against people with unusual, unconventional ideas. The show's purpose is to expose charlatans and support Truth in a forum that gives everyone their chance to support their ideas and beliefs. I expect it to be a very successful show, especially with William Pontius as the govern…er, moderator."

Judas knew of Pontius. He didn't like him, but he was a popular moderator; hardnosed, without compassion or mercy, a tear down kind of guy.

"Tell me more. When's the first show, who's on it and what's it about?"

"Have you seen the local news lately, about a Hispanic kid at showings of The Passion?"

"You mean Jesus! Yes, I have seen him. He got up and told the audience to leave and boycott the movie. Says it's misogynist, anti-Semitic and even antichrist. He sure has balls! He has a very novel, but quite sensible perspective on Christianity. He's got the name for what he's doing and I've even heard people say he's the real thing, Jesus come again."

"Do you think he is?" Mal fished.

"It's a bit far-fetched for me. Jesus didn't seem to save anyone his first time around and most Jews are still waiting for someone else. I'm not much into the savior thing anyway. My mother's always trying to save me, or feed me and I couldn't take any more saving. But then this Jesus fellow just seems to be saying that crucifixion isn't the way to God's Good Will."

"So, no I don't think he's the second coming, but I like him. I'd like to meet him."

"Excellent," beamed Mal, "because we want him to be the guy for our first show! And Pontius and I want you to bring him to tria…, er bring him onto the show."

"I've never met him. What makes you think he even wants an agent or wants to be on a show like yours. You just want to slam him!"

"We just want to give him his day in cour….er the spotlight, give him a bigger venue to share his views. And I have an intuitive hit that you, Judas, are just the one to bring him to us."

Judas sat silently for a moment. He knew what they wanted to do with Jesus, and he was reluctant to recruit him as a client, only to betray him and set him up for these wolves, yet there seemed a certain inevitability to what was happening.

He looked Mal in the eye and said with resolve, "OK, I'll see what I can do, but it's going to cost you. Public hangings don't come cheap and it's obvious your motives are less than honorable."

"We'll pay you well for delivering him to us," Mal sneered. "And don't be so self-righteous. We want Truth to be served, your kind are always only interested in the money. You can always be counted on to consider the count. That's why most of you are accountants!" At this clever bit of humor, Mal started to guffaw, got up and walked out the door.

He turned. "My card is there on your desk. Contact me when you get it arranged." Then he was gone.

Judas looked at the card. He felt strangely calm and peaceful considering the company he had just endured.

Somehow he knew he had done the right thing, was playing his part in a bigger play. His mother had taught him to be straight and truthful and he was determined to be just that. He would contact Jesus, tell him what he had been asked to do and warn him about the people he would be dealing with. Jesus could use the money as he chose and he would get as much out of these bastards as possible, knowing that it was only the money they valued, knowing they were projecting their greed onto him.

As Yogi Berra said, "deja vu all over again."

Chapter 15: The Signing

McCabe's was a large music store in Santa Monica where a musician could get whatever he or she needed. It was a rootsy, folksy, acoustic kind of place, guitars of all sorts lining the walls. In the back was a cozy theater where folk groups and singer/songwriters from all over the country came to perform. The people were friendly and professional, and everyone who went to a concert there always had a good time, leaving with a warm family feeling in their belly.

As a great fan of folk music, Judas had been there often. He loved the ambience and usually met a few friends whenever he went. This Saturday night he came to see a new group, Sibling Revelry, who played some sixties cover songs that he especially liked as well as some of their own music. Their theme was all about Peace and Brotherly/Sisterly Love, about coming together and getting off on the interconnectedness of all things. They also played a song about accountability, about fixing things ourselves and giving up the childish, magical thinking that someone or something outside ourselves would save us from ourselves; sensible, sane stuff.

The irony of the scene was not lost on Judas when the lead guitarist introduced the members of the band. There was Maria on percussion, Luke on bass, Marcus on fiddle, and Jesus, the lead guitarist, doing the introductions. Judas had come here, as per his agreement with Mal, to talk to Jesus about getting him on the show.

After the inevitable couple of encores, the four musicians mingled with the appreciative audience and Judas approached the confident, charismatic Jesus. He took an instant liking to the guy the moment he saw him come on stage, recognizing his presence and his pure pleasure in being with those around him. As he watched and heard him play, his liking turned to loving in a way he had never before experienced.

Jesus saw Judas approach and met him like he had known him always, eagerly offering his hand and grabbing his shoulder.

"You played the kind of music I most like to hear. I thoroughly enjoyed the concert," Judas said as their eyes met.

"Thanks," Jesus responded with a smile. "I noticed you in the audience and had this strong gut feeling to meet and talk to you. What's with that?"

"The belly knows best, I guess. I came here specifically to meet you and talk with you. My name is Judas. I run Judas' Chariot, a small actors' agency in Hollywood and I want to represent you and present you with an offer to appear on a new television show."

"You're not too comfortable with this proposal, are you?"

"I have mixed feelings. My discomfort is obvious isn't it? Well, that's good because I don't want to bullshit you or cloud your perceptions, as if that were possible now that I have met you."

"Go on," Jesus encouraged him.

"Basically, there's this rather slimy guy named Mal who is co-producing a new show with a well known commentator and producer named William Pontius. No, it's not a music show and it's not about your group. What I got from Mal, and he was intentionally vague, was that the show is about roasting people who have unconventional ideas and who are growing in popularity. He seemed to have a rather fanatical and one-pointed desire to sacrifice you first."

"What's in it for me," Jesus asked, obviously amused by the offer.

"It's a pretty big show, with some very wealthy sponsors, so you would be well paid for 'going down' in public. That's their intention, even though he didn't give me the how and why. The why was obviously personal; you may know more about it than I. I don't get from you that money is a major motive for what you do. You will also get to say your piece, or peace, to millions of people worldwide. If that appeals to you, and you think you can handle what the wolves want to do with you, I'll let them know and work out the details of the arrangement; then run them by you for your approval."

"I appreciate your honesty," Jesus said. "Do it and let me know what you arrange. Here's my number."

They shook hands and Jesus gave Judas a hug.

"I'm gonna find my guys and do some more mingling," Jesus said and disappeared into the crowd.

100

Judas turned and walked out of McCabe's into the brightness of the Santa Monica weekend night.

Chapter 16: The Pickets and The Kiss

November 1st, All Saints' Day, the Day of the Dead, Sun in Scorpio, and the first episode of "Exposed" was ready to go on the air. It was being filmed live and was a huge gamble for the producers and the sponsors, as anything could happen on live television.

Judas had come through for Mal, delivering up Jesus as the sacrifice for the show. At least, that was how Mal viewed it. Having met and talked with Jesus a few times, Judas wasn't so sure about who would be victim, who victimizer.

There had been a great deal of publicity and the crowds outside the studio waiting for the principal players were huge and electric with expectancy. All the seats had been sold out and hundreds had paid for standing room.

Three vans pulled up in front of the studio, all marked with large, eight pointed stars and the words, JEWS FOR JESUS in bold, black letters printed under the stars. Five men jumped out of each van and a sixth ran to the back, lifted the door, pulled out a bunch of picket signs and handed them out to the others, military style. Then they all lined up and began pacing back and forth in front of the crowds, yelling various slogans.

"Jesus was a Jew and will always be a Jew!"

"Jesus, not HeyZeus!"

"Jews say NO to Mexican Messiahs!"

"Mexicans aren't chosen, they're uncircumcised!"

Strangely, even though the picketing Jews for Jesus were all of different height and stature, they all had the same noses.

One of the guys in the crowd yelled out, "Hey, these guys all look like Adrian Brody! How come you guys all have the same noses?"

Another yelled, "You guys all go to the same plastic surgeon?"

"Hey, it's the Brody Bunch!" another right behind the pickets called out. "Get it? The Brody Bunch!" and he slapped one of them on the back. The 'Jew for Jesus' turned on the guy and hit him over the head with his sign. "Mishuguna asshole!" he said in a very poor imitation of a Yiddish accent.

The pickets continued marching and yelling, even at times pushing people out of the way.

Some security guards pushed forward, corralled the picketers and herded them off to the side at the same time that a limo pulled up. A page opened the door and William Pontius, the show host, stepped out and raised his hands to the cheering crowd. He loved this part and he played it to the hilt, bowing, gesturing and smiling like a Roman soldier ready for battle and conquest. Then he strode gallantly into the studio.

Another car, a hybrid, pulled up as Pontius' limo pulled away. Another page came forward and opened the doors. Jesus, Maria, Luke and Marcus climbed out of their seats and walked towards the studio doors. Paul hopped out of the back seat and trotted along behind, tail wagging with excitement.

"Just like the good old days," he thought as he stepped proudly, ears still dragging on the pavement.

"Sucker," Someone in the crowd called out.

"They're gonna eat you alive," another yelled.

"Hey," another screamed, "Jesus has a pet pooch. Our savior must carry a pooper scooper!"

The crowd liked that one and laughed derisively.

The Brody bunch, having broken loose from the guards, began pacing again and lined up on either side of Jesus and his friends, forcing them to walk the gauntlet, all the while bad-mouthing Mexicans, Hispanics, and women, and when they saw Luke and Markus, lesbians and gays.

"Look, he hangs out with gays and dykes," one shouted. "He can't be Jesus come again!"

Marcus turned and loudly responded. "Well, he IS Jesus and he hangs out with all kinds of people, except maybe schmucks like you. And how do you know Jesus' disciples back then weren't gay? They all left their wives to hang out with the guys, **didn't** they?"

The crowd, taking a liking to Marcus, gave him a round of
applause and, entertainer that he was, he acknowledged his
new following with a smile and a nod of his head.

Judas emerged from the studio and walked up to meet
Jesus. They met, shook hands and Judas kissed Jesus on
both cheeks in greeting. He bent down and gave Paul a pet,
then led the foursome into the theater, ushering them to
their respective places for the upcoming event.

The crowd quickly dispersed, those with tickets going
inside, planted hecklers and those without tickets,
disappearing into the night. The Brody bunch ditched their
signs and oozed inside.

Chapter 17: On The Air

"Jesus," the man said as he came into the make-up room. "The show goes on in ten. It's time."

He walked in front of the chair and Jesus saw that his eyebrows were tightly knitted and his jaw was clenched. The man's eyes were full of worry and concern for him as he was about to go before the whole country, probably the world.

"Are you OK?" the make-up man wondered out loud as he thought to himself, *"Going before that panel of pompous, self-righteous, know-it-alls. I'd rather hang out with the local street people."*

Jesus, reading his mind, laughed. "We're all local street people, no matter how we dress, no matter who we think we are. When I'm in situations like this, being with the "self-righteous ones" I imagine all of us just sitting together naked. It's amazing how the intimidation and false power fall away when the collar and the cross and all the so-called symbols of spiritual authority fall away."

The man led Jesus down a hallway and into the brightly lit stage area, Paul trotting happily at his heels. Jesus was seated in an unassuming and comfortable chair placed in the center of a semicircle. Paul circled three times and curled up contentedly at his feet. He sighed, put his head on his paws and closed his eyes.

Jesus made himself comfortable by tucking his left leg under his right thigh, yogi style, his spine straight. He closed his eyes and gently rolled his head around to loosen the tension in his neck. He checked in with his breathing and slowed his heart rate as he was accustomed to do in situations like this.

When he opened his eyes, he carefully took in the scene and the players involved. Across from him sat four men and one woman, each in a different type of chair, each dressed in an outfit that told the world who they thought they were.

On his far left, sitting in a large, high-backed, red velvet covered chair, sat a portly, middle-aged man with a very red face. The color of the chair intensified his ruddy complexion and Jesus felt an intuitive desire to fan him and offer him a cool cloth. He was bald on top with a spare circle of fine grey-brown hair that looked like a threadbare skirt wrapped around a very large, blushing egg. Atop the egg sat a little, round, red skullcap. His rimless glasses pinched the tip of his fleshy, pink nose and his head sat atop multiple chins that rested on and flowed over his black tunic and red robe. A large jeweled cross sat on his chest, the chain that held it disappearing under the lowest layer of neck. Except for the cross, he was dressed and looked much like a very well fed vampire. Jesus knew this was a Catholic cardinal (he was dressed like one of the colorful, red cardinal birds and he realized the bird must have been named for these clerics' red attire). Jesus' whole extended family was Catholic and there were pictures of the Pope in his grandparents' home. They believed in the Pope's connection to Jesus and God, the virgin birth and all that stuff. His grandfather even seemed to believe that his mom Maria was still a virgin.

107

"People are more interested and invested in manipulating events to support their beliefs than they are in actually discovering truth," he mused.

Jesus shuddered at the sight of the large cross. He did not like crosses. His experience with them was most unpleasant, most painful. Crosses were used to torture and kill people, not for wearing around necks. He could never understand the cross as a symbol of someone's love for him. To his perception, wearing a cross as a symbol of love was like hanging the gun someone used to kill your boy or girl friend around your neck. Jesus wouldn't even use a cross to keep a vampire away, he avoided going to church, and always got squeamish when at communion they talked about eating his body and drinking his blood.

"I love you Jesus, so I am going to wear a cross to remember always how much you suffered for me. I love you so much that I am glad you suffered instead of me." He shuddered again. He didn't like his loved ones (and that included all creation) to suffer and he certainly wouldn't commemorate over and over a painful experience that happened two thousand years ago.

"If these people had any love for me," he thought, *"they would stop crucifying me. Once was enough! And where they ever got the idea that my death was going to free them from the results of their heartless actions is beyond me."*

"These people need serious therapy."

To the right of the cardinal's throne sat a rather diminutive man in his middle years with very dark hair. Jesus noticed the hair first as it was so meticulously styled, set and dyed. There were absolutely no color variations and it appeared obsessively unnatural. This fellow was also dressed in a black suit and wore a black and white tie. On his right lapel was a button that read "First Chosen." Jesus couldn't find a single wrinkle and noticed the man was repeatedly smoothing his suit jacket and looking for lint or hairs, removing whatever blemishes he could discover. Any found hairs were doubtlessly not his own as his was tightly glued down. His eyebrows were also plucked and dyed to match.

The fellow seemed quite high strung, fidgeting in his seat, his eyes looking around anxiously. There was an uncanny and fanatical light flickering in his eyes and Jesus couldn't quite tell if he was smiling or sneering. Jesus wondered if the guy was rabid.

He sat in a rather modest, black leather arm chair. Everything about him was rather dark and he kept staring at Jesus as though he wanted to set him on fire. In his eyes was the "I know who you are and I will expose you" look.

Jesus knew this man was dangerous, yet he was also rather ludicrous and funny; *"insane"* he thought to himself.

In the center, directly across from Jesus, sat the show host and moderator William Pontius. He was also one of the show's producers and this was the first airing. This was Pontius' Pilot. If the show was well received and the ratings were good, Mr. Pontius' plan and pleasure was to put people he perceived as frauds, false prophets and spiritual charlatans in the chair to be grilled, eaten and exposed every week by his panel of religious "experts." He conceived of the idea when he researched the popularity of public torture and hangings of heretics during different times in history. Mal's idea to put this fellow Jesus, whose popularity was beginning to spread, on the hot seat for his pilot was a stroke of genius. Thousands of people were claiming Jesus as the Christ returned, celebrating his message of Peace and Accountability and basking in his charisma. Women and gay men were fantasizing about his good looks and incredible abs. Men and lesbian women were falling in love with Jesus' girl friend Maria Magdalena. And the Humane Society, animal psychics and therapists absolutely loved that Jesus traveled with a mongrel dog named Paul that Jesus seemed to love and talk to. No one had ever anticipated that a messiah would have a pet.

Pontius really didn't care whether Jesus was the Christ, the anti-Christ or just a young, sexy, charismatic Latino. He had washed his hands of the truth long ago. All he cared about was his show and his ratings. He was eager to put this kid in the chair and loose the angry and threatened "experts," on him; "experts" who were certain that he was either a fraud or the evil prince himself.

Pontius sat in the largest seat, a Roman-style, marble throne. He was wearing a flashy, sequined sport jacket, lots of gold jewelry and had an incredible handlebar moustache. He lived at Caesar's Palace in Vegas and had an unbelievable tan.

Jesus looked at Pontius and made eye contact.

110

Pontius shifted uncomfortably on his throne. He felt an uncanny and unpleasant sense of deja vu.

To the left of Pontius' marble throne, in a more modest and traditional armchair, sat a very well-dressed, rather slick-looking young man with a saccharin smile on his face. He was looking at Jesus with a "knowing" look, as though he had just sold Jesus a used car and they both knew he had given Jesus a great deal and he should be grateful. He was thin, well dressed in a conservative and impeccably pressed sharkskin suit, and his tie was knotted perfectly. He looked like the friendliest and most successful person Jesus had ever seen. Jesus wondered if the guy was human; if he ever farted in public.

Right next to the car salesman guy, perched at the edge of her seat and sitting poised, pert and pretty, was a very attractive blond woman. Jesus could feel her strength, power, and determination, as well as her "don't fuck with me'" attitude. She was dressed for success with the face of a country western singer. She seemed to be with the salesman guy as they kept looking at and to each other whenever anyone spoke.

She was his perfect "accessory."

"No, wait," Jesus realized, "he was HER perfect accessory."

Just then a stage director stepped in front of the set and yelled, "ready in 5, 4, 3…Action," and pointed to Mr. Pontius.

111

Pontius grinned at the central camera like the Cheshire Cat and began.

"Welcome, ladies and gentlemen, to this first presentation of "Exposed." It is our purpose to "Expose" to the world, the truths and falsehoods propounded by contemporary teachers and prophets of all subjects. In these tumultuous times, new personalities are popping up everywhere, full of answers (and full of themselves), challenging conventional wisdom and claiming they know better than the wise, successful and well established leaders of our society."

Here Pontius began cranking up his voice. He looked seriously at the audience (the cameras) and clenched his fists.

"We are here to separate the chaff from the wheat, to let the mud settle and separate the truth from the lies, to EXPOSE the liars and false prophets!"

"We are here to make sure that the frauds and the charlatans do not take advantage of you by offering their false hope and promises!"

"Everyday, someone claims they can do miracles, claims they have the answers, claims they can save us while all the while they just want our money!!!"

"But we know better, don't we!"

Pontius was now waving his arms and shouting. At the same time a stage hand held up a card telling the audience to clap, stamp and make loud noises.

The audience clapped, stamped their feet and responded with cheers, cat calls, whoops and hollers, then settled down and waited for their next instructions. Some of them yawned, as they had been in TV audiences before.

Paul, sleeping at Jesus' feet, lifted his head up and also yawned. He had done this whole thing himself back in the old days when he was a preacher. He had whipped up the emotions of both Jews and Gentiles, filling them with truths and righteousness. He knew all the answers (and even when he didn't he pretended he did. Doubt was very bad for business and the follower numbers always dropped when he didn't get his speech just right). He looked at Pontius, lifted his head slightly and emitted a low, sad, melancholy howl. Then he shook his big ears, farted loudly and went back to sleep.

"Tonight, my fellow seekers of the truth," Pontius continued with his introduction, "we have an esteemed council of theological authorities whose special expertise is in ascertaining and debunking false messiahs. These renowned scholars have been researching and assimilating the absolute truths revealed in the Old and New Testaments, especially as regards the authenticity of miracles and prophesies. They are here to guide us on the One True Path of Prophesy and Revelations and to PROTECT us from those who would have us find our own way!"

Here Pontius slammed his fist down hard on the arms of his marble throne and winced at the pain. He caught himself, looked up seriously and whispered in dramatic fashion into his microphone, "Imagine such arrogance."

Then he straightened his face and assumed the "friendly, authoritative, impartial, reporter, anchorman pose," looked thoughtfully at his audience, and continued in an even, deep, touching and concerned tone of voice.

"It is my honor to introduce our esteemed panel, all of whom are ready to EXPOSE the lies and REVEAL the truth. They are ready and eager to tell all of you where to go…"

"On my far right sits the venerable Cardinal Caldwell Cluck, humble and honorable shepherd of the flocks of the Holy Virgin Churches of the Undeflowered, and renowned at debunking inauthentic miracles. Cardinal Cluck has spent his entire life searching for evidence of the intactness of the Virginal Hymen and is the composer of numerous Hymns to the Hymen. He has co-authored the most comprehensive Hymen Hymnal ever published!"

Pontius looked at the audience, put his hands together and said, "Let's all suck it up for Cluck," and began making sucking noises.

The stage hand held up a sign which said, in big letters, MAKE SUCKING NOISES.

The audience all stood up and started puckering their lips, making sucking noises like they were all kissing someone's ass. Some of them couldn't quite get it and started making braying noises like donkeys in heat. The camera panned the audience and showed some of them turning red.

114

"Such passion," praised Pontius at the audience participation.

Paul groaned and covered his head with his paws.

Cardinal Cluck shook like a mound of strawberry Jell-O.

Jesus, looking at the audience in disbelief, was feeling a little quesy.

Cardinal Cluck jiggled some more and then burped.

Pontius continued with his introductions, gesturing with his right hand to the man next to him in the dark suit.

"Next to me on my right is the esteemed pastor of the 'All Aboard For Bliss Ministries,' and the author of the best selling book, Rapture or Rupture: Who Goes and Who Gets Left Behind to Suffer and Die a Painful, Lonely and Ignominious Death for All Eternity and Then Some, Timothy 'Take Me Home' TuDay."

Pontius furrowed his eyebrows to affect a very serious countenance, one of his favorite poses, and stared hard at the camera. His voice took on the tone of a sports announcer making a very important point.

"Pastor Tuday is the Rapture Raptor himself." His voice went up in volume. "He is The Eagle, Captain of the End Team," his voice picked up in volume and became as authoritative as he could make it. He was still working on this one so it wasn't perfected yet. "He is The Man who can coach YOU and choose YOU to join **Team Rapture**. All of you out there in these precarious times, listen carefully when this man speaks, and do not, I repeat, do **NOT** get **LEFT BEHIND!**"

Whereupon the stagehand held up a sign reading: "Rise and shout CHOOSE ME."

The audience jumped to their feet and began screaming, "CHOOSE ME, Tim, CHOOSE ME! Pick me up Great Eagle; pick me for YOUR TEAM!"

Others began chanting, "I won't stay, take me away, take me away Tuday! I won't stay, take me away, take me away Tuday! I won't stay, take me away, take me away Tuday!"

Suddenly hundreds of the audience rushed toward the stage with their arms raised, begging to be chosen screaming over and over again, "I won't stay, take me away, take me away Tuday!" Pandemonium seemed inevitable until Pastor Tuday himself held up a card that said,

> "Stop. The Time to Choose will come. Go back to your seats. Buy my Book at intermission."

Which everyone did and everyone will. He was used to this as it happened all the time.

Pontius straightened himself on his throne and cast a dignified look towards the well-dressed gentleman on his left. Gesturing with his left hand he continued his introductions.

"It is with great pleasure," he said proudly, "that I introduce the esteemed gentleman on my left. His ministry holds the current world record for followers and the wealth of his church is almost equal to that of the Vatican. As far as we can tell because no one knows how much treasure is socked away in secret places in the Vatican. Nevertheless, you gotta respect a man with so much wealth and so many followers. We just know his messages are righteous and worth listening to because it's impossible for so many of us to be wrong."

Pontius actually stood up and announced in a loud, gleeful voice: "People of the world, please welcome the Profit Bradley Doe Nation!"

At this the whole audience jumped up from their seats with wild applause (as the sign held by the stagehand prompted them to do), yelling "Profit, Profit, we want the Profit!"

Cardinal Cluck and Pastor Tuday looked a bit miffed and pissed at Pontius for standing up for Doe Nation's introduction.

Paul rolled over and played dead.

Doe Nation himself stood up stylishly, smiled stylishly and raised his right hand stylishly. Then he stylishly began to speak in a very smooth, silky and stylishly southern dialect.

The audience followed the next card's directions and stood quietly stunned.

"My beloved, fellow American Christians, and all of you fellow American Christian WannaBes throughout the world watching tonight, I bid y'all welcome." He lowered his head and smiled shyly, (and stylishly).

"Let us put our hands together and lower our humble heads in prayer."

The spotlight reflected off his exquisitely stylish suit and shone forth in a golden aura.

"Dear God, you are our provider. Man proposes and God disposes. Everything comes from You. We know that we are nothing and You are everything and so we ask You to give us everything we want, as a Good Father is wont to do for His beloved children."

"Father, we also know that it feels soooo good to give. It feels soooo good for me to be here to give Your wisdom and Your promises to my beloved flock and it feels soo good to give my flock the opportunity to feel soo good by giving everything they can to their wonderful church. And soo the goodness gets bigger and bigger."

"Father, you are the Most Rich and the Most Righteous and we are made in Your image. We therefore follow You, getting richer and more righteous every day."

"Father, we thank you for placing all the suffering in life on Your Son Jesus so that we do not have to feel the pain or responsibility."

118

"Jesus, you are our savior and we come to God's Kingdom through your sacrifice. We remember your suffering every day and give thanks it is you and not us who suffers."

"We open our hands and we open our pockets that You may fill them again and again for You have said to us, "ask and you shall receive."

"Amen."

The audience, silent with deep reverence, responded as One with a solemn, "Amen."

Bradley sat down and assumed a perfect, reverent, stylish pose and the audience followed.

Paul trotted unstylishly across the stage, lifted up his leg and pissed on Profit Bradley Doe Nation's perfectly pressed pant leg. The piss slid off like rain hitting a stylish, expensive raincoat and settled stylishly into the carpet below. Bradley leaned over and gave Paul a gentle, compassionate and stylish pet.

Paul looked up, growled and trotted back to lie at Jesus' feet. He looked once more at Bradley, sighed in resignation and closed his eyes.

Pontius did not like women very much. He found that they didn't take him very seriously and he always felt somewhat petty in their presence. His shrink told him it had to do with the fact that his mother said he was a jerk. Jerk or not, it was his show now and even though Doe Nation insisted on his wife's presence on the show, he was not going to let her get him down.

"Women have no place in religious discussions," he thought to himself. *"They're only concerned with the here and now and have no concept of transcendence. They also have difficulty with the hierarchical order of things and think they are just as good as everyone else. Imagine!"*

He pulled in his disapproval and distaste, put on his patronizing face, and continued with his introductions.

"Last but not least," he began, "we are honored to present the first lady of Christian Ministries and the lovely wife *(it was hard for him to keep his upper lip from sneering when he said the word "wife")* of the gentleman next to her, Mrs. Bambi Nation."

The crowd clapped politely. No card was held up.

Bambi smiled sweetly, shifted in her seat and coyly slipped the hem of her skirt a few inches higher, showing a good deal of her thighs, exposing the smooth, naked flesh above the top of her silk stockings and below the lacy fringe of her intimate apparel.

Suddenly the audience started to hoot and holler and whistle with excitement. Cardinal Cluck, who was now staring at Bambi, had wondered about her hymen since she was on stage. He turned a brighter shade of red as his red robe rose between his legs.

120

Bambi was looking at Jesus flirtingly and Jesus felt his cock start to rise. *"That's power!"* he thought to himself.

Paul trotted over and started to hump her leg. The audience went wild with ecstasy!

Bambi, eyes still on Jesus, leaned over and scratched Paul's ears, then gently released him from her leg. He looked at her with longing, trotted back to his spot and began licking his extended red organ. He wanted to sing "Great Balls of Fire," but it came out only as a doggy sigh of desire and longing.

Pontius, pissed but not surprised, held up a card that read "Shut Up and Sit Down."

Everyone did.

Getting his control back, Pontius stood up and walked over towards Jesus. He looked down at him with the look of a lawyer circling a guilty man, of a vulture eying road kill. *"Thank You, God,"* he thought, *"for answering my prayers."*

"Our guest today," he spoke to the cameras, "is a very brave *(stupid)* young man who calls himself Jesus. There are many who are claiming that he is the same Jesus, come again to tell us of his Father's wishes for all of humanity. Although he has not claimed this himself, neither has he made any denials."

Pontius continued as though he was giving opening remarks to the jury at Jesus' trial.

"We are here today to judge this man and these claims. He will be given an opportunity to make a brief, opening statement and then our esteemed panel of experts *(and one woman)* will question him extensively with the intent to discover whether he is for real or just another fraud. We are here to EXPOSE falsehood and UPHOLD truth."

The stagehand appeared again and everyone held up their arms just like Pontius and chanted "EXPOSE, EXPOSE, EXPOSE."

Pontius held up his hand for silence, gestured to the audience, and continued.

"Then you, the people, will judge this man via our patent pending Fraudometer. So, without further ado, let the games begin…right after a short break and message from our sponsor."

After a short message from a friendly pharmaceutical company about improving your life with anti-depressants, the director held up his hand for the countdown to the show's resumption. When his last finger went down, he pointed to Pontius that he was now live on camera once again.

"Welcome once again, seekers of the truth, to EXPOSE. We are delighted to introduce you to our guest. His name is Jesus Christo Alvarez and he comes from the small desert town of Barstow, California. You may have heard of him as his name has appeared often lately in the media and many are proclaiming him as the Christ returned. We think it only fair that he be given the opportunity to express his views

122

and purposes to the people of the world and then subject his proclamations to the scrutiny of our Theological Authorities. As was the case on his first visit to Earth (Pontius couldn't help but smirk as he said this), it is up to the people at large to accept him or reject him as the Messiah."

He then gestured to Jesus with one hand and toward the camera with the other.

"I give you Jesus Christo Alavarez."

Paul, upon hearing his best friend's name, sat up and looked expectantly at Jesus. The audience and the panel of experts also looked expectantly, and in some cases, hungrily, at the young man in jeans sitting in the "hot" seat. With all the hoopla over the earlier introductions, it was as if he had disappeared. Now everyone looked at him as if seeing him for the first time. The set was silent. Everyone waited.

Jesus looked out at the audience quietly and slowly. He smiled. He then turned his gaze on his inquisitors, making eye contact where he could, avoiding it where he needed to (lest the bulge in his pants grow larger), and smiled again. He gave Paul a gentle pet, stood slowly and gracefully, and began his opening statement.

"I have said my piece before, and I really don't have anything else to add. So, I am going to let Paul here, who in a previous life had so many answers and so much to say on my behalf speak for me."

He turned to Paul who trotted over obediently, tail tucked in nervously. He bent over and whispered something in his big, floppy ear; then stood up and smiled again.

"I would like to introduce you to my good friend and teacher Paul, who will give you an opening statement."

Paul looked up adoringly at Jesus with his big, round, sad and wise Basset Hound eyes. Then he trotted to the front of the stage and looked adoringly at the audience. He lifted his head up and let out a long, sustained and sorrowful howl. Then he trotted over to the esteemed panelists, made the same statement to them, turned and looked again at Jesus.

Jesus crossed his hands over his heart and smiled contentedly. "Thank you, Paul, for your most profound wisdom. You speak clearly and truthfully the very words our Father has given you to speak. God as dog."

Jesus then recited some poetry.

"If you can't see God in All,
Then you can't see God at all."

Yogi Bhajan

"He prayeth best who loveth best
All things both great and small.
For the one true God who loveth us,
He made and loveth all."

Samuel Taylor Coleridge
"The Rhyme of the Ancient Mariner"

124

Jesus returned to his seat with Paul following behind. They both made themselves comfortable and waited for the show to continue.

After another, not so short, commercial break promoting more pills for more problems, Pontius again addressed the cameras and studio audience. "Our first question period will come from Cardinal Cluck." He gestured to the Cardinal on his right and said, "Cardinal Cluck, you're up."

The Cardinal hoisted his huge body out of his Holy Seat, shook his robes into place and felt anxiously to be sure his little red hat sat atop his round red head. He shuffled slowly over toward Jesus, head in the lead, bulky body following, looking like a giant turtle with a nasty sunburn. He stood before Jesus, then bent over and, holding the rim of his glasses, peered into his face while breathing heavily.

Jesus diplomatically slid his chair back, reached into his pocket, pulled out a tin of Altoids Wintergreen Mints, and offered one to the Cardinal.

The Cardinal grunted and shook his jowls back and forth. He looked away from Jesus out towards the audience and struck an authoritative pose. Then he turned abruptly toward him and pointing his finger with an accusatory gesture and mocking voice asked, "Are you Jesus Christ?"

Jesus looked up at him with a gentle smile and simply said, "yes."

"Harrumph," coughed the Cardinal, as he waved his hand in dismissal, "how do you know?"

"My mother gave me my name" Jesus said.

"And do you claim to have been conceived by the Holy Spirit?"

"Yes, definitely," Jesus replied. "My father and mother often spoke about their love for me and how that love resulted in my conception. How were your parents getting along when the Spirit moved them to invite you into this life?"

Cluck choked at this question and reddened a bit before waving it aside like a bruised piece of fruit. "I ask and you answer," he blubbered tersely.

The stagehand held up a sign telling the audience to laugh and call out, "One up for Cluck!"

Cluck, his face aligning itself into a big smirk, continued: "Is your mother a virgin?"

"No, of course not, that's not how it works. The Creator of this world set it up so that a man and a woman enj…"

"Enough, gulped the Cardinal, enough! We do not need your crass description of the sinful act of fornication to know immediately that you are a fraud. We ALL know from the Bible that Jesus was born of the VIRGIN Mary, conceived by the Holy Spirit, and not by the common, degraded union of a man and a woman!"

The Cardinal, considering himself both victorious and finished, shuffled back towards his seat, his face filled with

126

both triumph and disdain. Again, according to the script, the audience laughed and pointed their fingers at Jesus chanting, "fraud, fraud, a loser and a fraud."

"You are mistaken." Jesus said quietly.

The audience became silent and the Cardinal stopped in his tracks. He turned to Jesus, face livid. "What did you just say?" he hissed.

Jesus smiled graciously at him. "I said, my friend, that you are mistaken. There is no shame in being mistaken."

Jesus continued. "First, you base your 'knowledge' on a book that has been translated and reinterpreted and spoken and respoken and written and rewritten thousands of times. This knowledge is as dependable as the myriads of humans who have done this. You, a dedicated authority, scholar and devout historian (Cluck preened a bit at this part), cannot even agree with the biblical interpretations of your fellow Cardinals, so how can you be so sure. And the Bible does not even say that Mary remained a virgin after she told the angel that she was. The angel simply said, 'The Holy Spirit will come upon you, and the power of the Most High will overshadow you.' What does this mean? It could mean many things. It could mean that God Himself descended, came upon Mary in some form and fucked with her. It sure sounds like someone was lying on top of her, probably Joseph. My guess, and all we can do with the Bible is guess, is that Joseph was inspired by the Holy Spirit of Love and Reproduction and he impregnated Mary who was probably a virgin until then. Does not the Bible (since we are all forced to play Bible games because it seems your only source of belief and misunderstanding) say that we were created in the image of God? If this is true, and you say everything in the Bible is true, then God must also have a cock and must also like sex and, since He is the Great Senore' and the Source of all creation, I bet His Cock is quite something. No doubt Joseph had one hell of a Holy Hard-on and Mary was indeed FILLED with the Holy Spirit."

Jesus paused a moment, closed his eyes and made a blissful sound as he imagined their coming together.

He continued. "No living creature in God's entire creation reproduces without some sort of sex. The creatures have sex because they like it, it feels good. If it didn't feel good, no new creatures would be born because all the parents would find something else to do that's more fun, like bowling or playing baseball. I love baseball, but when my Maria Magdalena feels the urge and looks over at me, my other bat rises and balling her takes precedence over playing ball."

"If God has created us like Him, and He loves us and He loved Mary and chose her to birth His son, why would he want her to experience all the trials and tribulations of childbirth without any of the pleasure?"

"Why do you conceive of God as a Supreme Bastard and Bully, Someone who has Mary impregnated with a son without sex who He is going to forsake later on and have him killed so the rest of humanity can fuck their brains out, go to confession and then go to Heaven? Sounds pretty nuts to me."

128

By this time, the Cardinal looked like a volcano ready to explode. He was redder than ever and shaking violently and he was squeezing his cross so hard his hands began to receive the stigmata.

The audience was also agitated, some squirming as much as the Cardinal and some looking at Jesus with real interest, thinking that what he was saying actually made sense, perhaps more sense than what they had unquestionably always believed.

Jesus went on, "So, yes, I am Jesus Christo Alvarez and no, my mother Maria is definitely NOT a virgin and I am not some freak born of no sex. And only someone lost to reality would believe and defend the idea that the Jesus born 2000 years ago was conceived or born any differently than you or I."

"My questions to you, and to all others who believe in the Virgin story, is this: Why do you deny Holy Sexuality? Why are you so afraid of and so condemnatory of the sexuality created by God Himself?"

Cardinal Cluck had retreated to his red seat and was melting into his chair, sweating and shrinking anxiously away from this questioning that had become so offensive and disturbing.

Jesus walked slowly and gently over to the Cardinal and knelt on the stage in front of the Cardinal's throne. He took his hand, looked into his now very fearful eyes, and spoke in a most loving tone.

"My dearest Cluck, you've been a schmuck. You, most of all, need a good fuck."

The entire set and audience were dumbstruck and silent. Only the whirring noise of the cameras could be heard.

"You're obsessed with sex and think and wonder only about vaginas and whether they are open or closed. Your whole life is a condemnation of that which you most desire and that which your Father wants you to have. In your fear, you have even hidden your cock in folds of flesh, and hidden your flesh in the folds of your robes. You, and those like you, have chosen red thinking it powerful, yet it is the color of your shame and your embarrassment, the color of your anger towards woman who has the power to make you feel things you have decreed (even God doesn't know why) forbidden."

"Were you hurt so badly when you were young and in love that you have made your rejection, shame and hurt into a religion?"

"Come here with me dear Cluck to the back of the stage and *I* will hear *your* confession. Come and let me set you free."

Jesus took the Cardinal's shaking hand and rose with him, leading him from his chair towards a bench at the back of the stage, outside the range of the cameras and microphones. Paul followed behind and sat himself between them and the others on stage, keeping guard so that they would not be disturbed. Cardinal Cluck was shaking and weeping; rivulets were running down the sides

130

of the volcano, beginning to cool him, quelling the immanent eruption. They sat together, facing each other, Jesus still holding his hand, the Cardinal's head bent in humility and sorrow before the young Jesus.

The audience sat still and peaceful and in awe of the miracle taking place before them. Tears also streaked their cheeks as they watched and waited. They kind of wished they were watching Oprah or Jerry Springer, because then they would have been able to hear what was going on, but they respected the Cardinal's privacy.

Pontius rose and went up to Jesus, protesting his rude disregard of the show's format, complaining that the world TV audience had nothing to see or hear. Jesus waived him aside and told him to show another commercial about another pill that would solve another problem. Red-faced and furious, Pontius returned to his seat and, fuming, called for another word from their sponsor.

Jesus spoke gently to the Cardinal. "Dearest Father, you are truly a holy man for you have pledged your life trying to help others think of our Father. You have simply been mistaken and misled by your pain, as have many others. No one can hear you now but me. Tell me your story, share your pain with me and I will help you to free yourself."

Cardinal Cluck began to cry openly and convulsively, no longer able to hide his pain and sorrow. He buried his head on Jesus' breast and sobbed and sobbed and sobbed.

Jesus placed his hand on the back of Cluck's head and held him tenderly.

131

Gradually the Cardinal stopped shaking and sobbing and began to catch his breath. His breathing slowed and a quiet peace settled over him. He lifted his head and looked into Jesus' gaze with a deep trust. He began his story.

"Her name was Mary and she was the most beautiful, wonderful girl I ever knew. I was only sixteen. I was a fat, ugly kid with pimples and spent my life mostly alone, wishing I could be someone else. I would fantasize about being with Mary all the time the way a sixteen year old fantasizes about girls. You know what I mean?"

Jesus replied with understanding: "Sure, thinking about her made you feel good between your legs. Every healthy guy feels those things and fantasizes about sex. Did you have any friends, other guys you could share your feelings with, so you could know you were mostly like every other guy your age?"

The Cardinal continued: "I hung out with a couple of other dorky guys, but when I told them how I liked Mary, they laughed at me and told me I didn't have a chance with someone like that. Besides, they said even if I could get close to her, I wouldn't have a clue about what to do. They were both right and wrong. My body knew what to do but my mind was tormented. I was raised in a strict, Catholic home and went to a Catholic high school. I was racked with guilt all the time. Every time I saw her, I felt both lust for her body and guilty over thoughts that I was violating her."

"The lust always triumphed over the guilt and after imagining having sex with her numerous times everyday (I lived much of my life locked in the bathroom), I actually

132

got up enough nerve to ask her over to my house to watch a movie together on a night my parents would be gone. Amazingly, she smiled at me and said that sounded like fun."

"I told my "friends" and they were also amazed, but they continued to make jokes about how she was just feeling sorry for me and that I still wouldn't know what to do with a girl if she was laying next to me stark naked."

"Well, Mary came over and we sat together, watching a horror movie I had rented. I sat next to her full of anxiety and ambivalence. My friends were right. I really didn't know what to do. I put my arm around her and pulled her to me and tried to kiss her. She laughed and pushed me away, saying she had a crush on another guy and just wanted to be my friend. I got more agitated and tried to pull her down again but she pushed me away again and got up to leave. I was angry and hurt and just sulked. She was also angry and told me I was creepy and left in a hurry. I felt like a complete idiot. I was hurt and wanted to hurt her even though she had not done anything wrong."

"I watched the rest of the movie together with my resentful, revengeful mind, plotting a way to both hurt Mary and prove to my friends what I couldn't even prove to myself. After an adequate amount of time, I went over to the house where my friends were hanging out, puffed up my chest and sauntered in like some fat cock, proclaiming that we had "done it." They looked at me with disbelief but after some questioning on their part and bragging on mine, I seemed to have convinced them and they gave me some reluctant and envious congratulations."

"Now I was both a dork and a liar. I never felt so shitty or phony in my life and, believe me, shitty and phony were always constant companions. I had locked myself into perpetual pretense. I was damned!"

"Go on," Jesus encouraged, full of interest and concern without judgment.

"Of course my 'friends' broadcast the news throughout school and Mary, despite her protestations that I was a creep and a liar, began to be viewed by others in ways she certainly wasn't. Other creeps would approach her and tease her. I, supreme creep that I was, (still am), stuck to my story, digging myself further down into hell."

"Gradually the whole episode faded as other concerns eclipsed the petty drama I had created. No one really cared whether I had "done it" or not. Those I had convinced didn't care and those who didn't believe me also didn't care. Mary learned who her friends really were. She got into a relationship with a really great guy who knew she hadn't been sexual with me simply because he believed her, and he respected her wish to remain a virgin until she was sure about "doing it.""

"Her guy approached me one day when I was alone and told me that he knew I was a liar and he knew I knew I was a liar. He told me he loved Mary and that I was the scum of the earth and if I continued to lie about Mary, or any other girl, he would beat the shit out of me."

"I never said another word about it to anyone, but I never owned up to the truth either. I never apologized to Mary."

134

Cardinal Cluck began again to sob quietly.

"Instead, I sanctified my shame, blaming my body and my sexuality rather than confronting and healing my duplicitous mind. Oh God, I see how I have wrapped my sin in my religion, like a pig in a blanket, hiding it from the world and myself."

"Yes," Jesus said quietly, "you have wrapped your dysfunction and uncleanliness in your religious habit. It is a very unworkable and unhealthy habit. What are you going to do?"

Cluck took a deep breath and looked at Jesus.

"I have never shared this with anyone. I just figured I could atone for what I did by lying to myself some more; by pretending to be someone who has transcended the "lower passions," all the while obsessing about sex by condemning it. You are right, I am mistaken and my life has been a sham."

"And how do you feel right now," Jesus asked.

Cluck paused a moment to check in with himself.

"Actually," he said somewhat surprised, "I feel better than ever. I feel exposed, vulnerable and open. The truth of my life has been a burden I have hidden from myself. What has changed is that it is no longer hidden and so I can do something about it. I feel lighter and have a personal sense of purpose that is both humble and my own, instead of Holy and full of shit."

"I am going to write a letter to Mary and find out where she is. If possible I will send her the letter and tell her I am sorry. If I cannot get it to her for whatever reasons, I will be writing it for myself anyway, for it is my life I have ruined and wasted."

"I am going to resign my position as Cardinal and leave the holy order, for there is nothing holy about what I represent. I am going to go on a diet and find a good therapist so I can reconnect with my body and find out what is healthy. By God, I am going to create a new life that is not based on lies!"

"Good plan," Jesus agreed, "and be patient with yourself. When you are ready, you will find a girl like Mary and you will fall in love. Then you will know and truly experience the Holy Spirit. Oh, and I recommend the Subway diet. A good, thick six-incher is all that you need, if you get the point." Jesus smiled as he never ceased to amaze and amuse himself.

Jesus took Mr. Cluck's hand and raised him up from where he sat. He hugged him and led him back to his seat. Cluck sat up straight, removed his scull cap and took his cross off from around his neck. He looked out confidently at the stunned and silent audience, gestured toward Jesus who had quietly returned to his seat and said: "This man, whose name is Jesus, is truly my best friend."

Paul jumped up in front of Jesus, barking and wagging his tail. The entire audience followed Paul's lead with loud and heartfelt applause. Not so much for what Jesus had done, but for what all could sense Cluck had become!"

After what was touted as the new record for the network's longest commercial break, the cameras returned to the show's host. Pontius, having composed himself and feeling a little better after he heard how happy his sponsor was at all the free ad time and their verbal commitment to sponsor at least six more shows (with equal ad time at the same discount of course), smiled into the cameras and spoke.

"Welcome back to 'Exposed,' where Truth reigns supreme and frauds come clean. And we want everyone to know that Cardinal Cluck has been wiping his tears away with extra soft Lament With Us tissues from our favorite pharmaceutical sponsor. Lament With Us tissues are infused with time release anti-depressants sure to raise your spirits! And even after you stop crying, use these tissues to apply and remove your make-up, to blow your nose, even to clean your ears. That way your spirits will always be raised and depression will become a thing of the past. (Sponsors note, use of these tissues may adversely affect your sex life and are highly recommended for priests and other people of the cloth.)"

Jesus looked over at Cluck and motioned for him to put the tissues down. Paul, with an approving nod from Jesus, sauntered over to the Cardinal's chair, picked up the box of tissues and carried them offstage. *"Gotta read those labels,"* Jesus mused.

Pontius continued: "Our next panel member to present questions to our guest and words of wisdom to the world is our expert on Revelations, the Rapture and the End of Days, Pastor Timothy "Take Me Home" Tuday." Pontius gestured towards the man in black on his right and said, "You're up, Tim."

Timothy jumped to his feet, full of energy and excitement, and skipped past Jesus to the front of the stage. He wanted to talk to the world and acted as though Jesus wasn't there.

Jesus thought he looked like a dancing undertaker ready to take under everyone with his longing for destruction. He couldn't suppress the cold shiver that ran through his body as Tuday passed by.

Looking down at the people in the audience with a stern and disapproving glare, Tuday raised both hands above his head and began.

"The Day of Reckoning will soon be upon us. Will you be ready?"

The audience stirred uncomfortably in their seats and people looked at one another nervously.

"WILL YOU BE READY?!"

One member of the audience timidly stammered, "ye…yes."

A stage hand held up a card saying "Yes, yes, I will be ready!"

The rest of the crowd, more comfortable now that they knew what to do, began shouting "Yes, yes, I will be ready, I will!"

Tuday continued: "The signs are everywhere. The unbelievers are attacking Holy Jerusalem and the day of the Anti-Christ is fast approaching. War and pestilence is on the rise and there will be destruction and pain like never before as the sinful ones run rampant over the earth. AIDS, Avian Flu, Tuberculosis, drought and floods, terrorism and nuclear conflagration are all signs that the end of days is upon us."

"And we who have chosen Christ and been chosen by Christ should rejoice at this destruction."

"Why, you might ask? Why should we rejoice over such events? Is that Christian behavior?"

"Rejoice because this destruction is God's Will and God's Plan. This is God's preparation for Jesus' Return, for the destruction of the unholy and the Triumph of the Holy!"

Tuday bent forward towards the audience and began pointing his finger at different people. "And you, you are either with us or against us!"

He stood up tall, jutted his chin out and whispered like the trumpet of doom, "Are you with us, or against us?"

The audience was transfixed, mouths hanging open, drool dripping down chins.

Tuday then turned on Jesus who was sitting calmly and quietly in his seat, filing his nails with an emery board.

"And you," he screamed and pointed at Jesus. "Yes, you, you are a fraud and a demon. You cannot be Jesus come again because, according to all the prophecies, you are here too soon! The anti-Christ has not yet come as ruler of Europe and you will not appear for three and a half years after that. That alone exposes you as an imposter!"

Tuday began to laugh hysterically. "What," he said to Jesus as he hyperventilated, "do you have to say to that?"

Jesus put his emery board into his shirt pocket and blew the dust from his nails. He calmly looked up at Pastor Tuday and said quietly, "Mark Twain said, 'It isn't what we don't know that causes problems. It is what we know for sure that ain't so that causes trouble.'"

"What's that supposed to mean?" Tuday asked derisively.

"It means," Jesus said as he stood and walked up to Tuday, "you have the mentality of a mass murderer."

Tuday looked as though someone had punched him in the stomach. "I beg your pardon," he said incredulously.

Jesus continued: "You think like a mass murderer and worse, for you would have God do your killing for you."

Tuday pulled himself up defiantly and replied, "I am a Christian. I am encouraging all people to follow the Word of God as written in the Bible, in Revelations."

"The Word of God," said Jesus, turning away from Tuday towards the audience and the cameras, "is the Creation itself. I am a Word of God, you are a Word of God, every man, woman and child, whether they consider themselves Christian, Muslim, Jewish, Buddhist, Atheist are all God's Words. The animals and plants, rocks, soil, oceans, deserts are all Words of God. *All this* is God's Language."

He turned back to face Tuday. "You are eagerly anticipating and encouraging the destruction of God's Words to support your beliefs in the perverted words of man. You are among the fanatics of every religion who place belief above the sanctity of life. God created life, man creates beliefs about life. Which is more important? Which is sacred?"

Jesus spread his arms wide, inviting Tuday in as he asked, "Why are you so anxious for the deaths of those who think and live differently? Why do you think that the Word of God that you are is a better word than others? Why do you engage in Mass Destructive Sibling Rivalry with your brothers and sisters?"

"You were directed to be your brother's keeper, giving your life to care for others, whether they are like you or different. If you want to be with Jesus, then act like Jesus and give your life in loving service to Life, not some misguided, harmful beliefs."

Jesus moved so that he could speak directly to Tuday and to the audience.

"Be Forgiving. For Giving. You, I, we are all for giving ourselves to life, not for wishing for our brothers' and sisters' destruction if they don't join our team."

141

Tuday looked bewildered. He too opened his arms to question. "But what about Revelations, what about the prophecies and the rapture? John said that Jesus said…"

"Life," Jesus continued in his strong, yet quiet voice, "does not end, though you be so eager for conclusions. Ask yourselves why and how you came to your conclusions. Ask yourself why you choose to believe and apply to today the ranting of men thousands of years ago who declared the world would end shortly. (See appendix A for descriptions of previous prophecies of doom that never came to pass). This planet has been here for millions of years and has endured through every doomsday prophesy of some God's final punishment."

Jesus' voice intensified. "And contrary to what you want to believe, neither I nor my Father, OUR FATHER, want this world to end. Neither does He want any of His children, our brothers and sisters, to suffer, no matter what we believe or where we live."

"You, like most everyone in this world, ennoble and deify suffering. You have imagined and created blood-thirsty gods; Christian, Jewish, Hindu, Muslim, and you feed them with your wars and sacrifices. What if instead we deified Joy? Harmony? Compassion? What kind of world would we live in if we created a God of Joy, a God of Peace? A God of Music perhaps?!"

Upon saying this, the theater began to vibrate with the beat of Reggae music coming from behind a curtain that wasn't there before. The panel members turned around in surprise, Pontius being the most surprised of all, since he supposedly

142

knew what was going to happen on his own show. The people in the audience began to move their feet, then rock their shoulders back and forth, looking at each other in pure glee. *"What an awesome show,"* they thought, and then they all jumped up from their seats and began dancing in pure ecstasy!

Jesus, as surprised as everyone else and always open to the Mystery of the Happening called Life, raised his arms, swaying and dancing around the stage, inviting all the religious "experts" to join him, reluctant as they were to appear "foolish." Even Paul was up on his hind legs, dancing like Snoopy, head up and howling in glee!

When everyone was up and bouncing, the curtain that wasn't there before rose up and there, playing a multitude of heavenly instruments, was a reggae band like no one had ever seen or heard before. It seemed like there were hundreds, no, thousands of musicians; men and women, young and old, from every culture, every race. Children too played horns and kazoos, drums and tambourines, all dancing around merrily. The people and instruments kept changing, appearing and disappearing, all except for one fellow in the center. He was a big, young, absolutely gorgeous Black Man with dreadlocks shooting from His Head like shooting stars in a dark, summer sky. He WAS The Dance, He WAS The Music. He wore white, baggy pants and a white T-shirt with letters and words that began to form sentences across His Chest. As they appeared, the music grew downright jolly, becoming both Music and Laughter. The Man Himself was laughing and laughing and laughing.

As each sentence appeared, everyone had their eyes on His Chest and, in unison, in time to the music, everyone read out loud:

"A Short Guide to Comparative Religions

Then spontaneously, half the audience cried out the name of the religion and the other half answered with how the shit goes down.

TAOISM	**Shit happens.**
BUDDHISM	**If shit happens, it's not really shit.**
ISLAM	**If shit happens, it's the will of Allah.**
PROTESTANTISM	**Shit happens because you don't work hard enough.**
JUDAISM	**Why does this shit always happen to us?**
HINDUISM	**This shit happened before.**
CATHOLICISM	**Shit happens because you're bad.**
HARE KRISHNA	**Shit happens rama rama.**

T.V. EVANGELISM	**Send more shit.**
ATHEISM	**No shit.**
JEHOVAH'S WITNESS	**Knock, knock, shit happens.**
HEDONISM	**There's nothing like a good shit happening.**
CHRISTIAN SCIENCE	**Shit happens in your mind.**
AGNOSTICISM	**Maybe shit happens, maybe it doesn't.**
EXISTENTIALISM	**What is shit, anyway?**
STOICISM	**This shit doesn't bother me.**
RASTAFARIANISM	**Let's smoke this shit.**

Jesus danced over in front of the "Band" and looked The Man in the eye. The Man smiled, winked and disappeared in a cloud of aromatic smoke. The whole band was gone! Jesus stood where he was before in front of Timothy Tuday. It was as if nothing had happened, except for a lingering rhythm and melody still softly sounding in everyone's ears. Only Paul kept howling and dancing around the stage until he realized that no one else was

145

listening anymore, or perhaps he was again imagining things. Sheepishly (it isn't necessary to be a sheep to act sheepishly), he came down onto all fours and returned to his place at the foot of Jesus' chair.

Jesus continued where he had left off, speaking in all seriousness and trying to stifle his continuing impulse to chuckle.

"None of John's incomprehensible prophecies that were 'soon' to come to pass have come to pass, and all your interpretations are only speculative, death-wishful thinking. Nor will any of them come to pass unless you make them, through your mass murder mentality, your self fulfilling prophesies. For you there will only be disaster, because no one is going to come and save you, no one is going to take you away in rapture. If any creatures deserve to be saved and spared the destruction you create, they are all the innocent animals and plants, and all the women and children who are always the victims of your religious wars. Fortunately or unfortunately for them, and for you, there will be no rapture, as our Father created us with the intelligence and free will to create either heaven on earth or hell on earth, and the choices you make will affect all creation."

Jesus looked out over the audience, and then looked directly into Tuday's eyes and said, "There is still time to choose, so I suggest you forget the rapture, stop waiting for a savior, and stop blaming your actions on God. Turn your weapons into plowshares and get yourself an electric car, for your fate is in your own hands!"

146

Jesus then took Timothy Tuday's hands into his own, opened them and held them palms up, and with the softest and kindest of voices asked, "Why is it so important to you that you be chosen above and before anyone else? And why would you have so many be left behind to suffer?"

Tuday started to pout and looked down at his feet. "No one ever chose me, for anything," he said in a pained and resentful voice.

"Tell me," Jesus invited.

"I was always invisible at home. I could have died and no one would have even noticed. At school I was never picked for any team. I would stand there while kids were chosen and the game would start and I would still be standing there. I hated it, I hated everyone, I wanted them all to die."

"I went to a revival and I was chosen. I called out Jesus' name loud and clear and I was accepted and seen and respected. I learned to prophesy and others wanted ME to choose them! Can you imagine what that felt like, to be Captain of the Team?!"

"You just wanted to play didn't you?" Jesus asked.

"I wanted to belong," Tuday said quietly.

Jesus put his arms around him and said, "You are a son of God and my brother. You were chosen to take part in this creation before the beginning of time and you can never be excluded. You know how it feels to believe you have been left out. Be sure that no other being, no matter how different, has to feel the pain of separation you have felt. Choose everyone and you will know you are chosen."

Then rapture infused every cell of Tuday's body as Jesus and he embraced and he began to glow with a sweet, golden light. The rapture spread to the entire audience and each person turned and hugged their neighbor. Everyone felt their combined hearts vibrate with an angelic music that sang, "Love your neighbor as yourself," and rapturous tears fell from many an eye.

Timothy Tuday then returned to his seat feeling a peace he'd never before known. He looked out at the audience with a love he'd never before felt. He was now truly chosen, just like everyone else. Paul walked over to him, jumped into his lap, licked his face and curled up peacefully for a nap.

While Paul was sleeping, he had a dream of Jesus speaking to his disciples and others on the Mountain. Jesus was standing powerfully and serenely saying, *"When you pray, you are not to be like the hypocrites; for they love to stand and pray in the football stadiums and on the television so that they may be seen by men. Truly I say to you, they have their reward in full.*

But you, when you pray, go into your inner room, close your door and pray to your Father who is in secret, and your Father who sees what is done in secret will reward you.

And when you are praying, do not use meaningless repetition as the actors do, for they suppose that they will be heard for their many words. So do not be like them; for your Father knows what you need before you ask Him."

148

Paul was snoring peacefully until the harsh sound of
Pontius' voice woke him up. He growled in distaste,
jumped from Tim's lap and trotted back to Jesus' feet.

"Mr. Doe Nation, you're up," Pontius grunted impatiently,
not at all pleased with what was going down and wanting to
move past all this unpleasant and unexpected, new-age,
touchy-feely stuff.

Bradley Doe nation tried not to listen to much of what
Jesus said to Pastor Tuday. He didn't like Tuday much,
didn't like the way he dressed. He would have picked
Tuday's pocket, but would never pick him for his team. He
also didn't want to listen because he had become preoccupied with the stain on his pants' leg, a delayed reaction
from Paul's earlier baptism. He didn't like performing in
front of an audience unless his dress was perfect and the
little spray can of spot remover he always carried with him
for such emergencies was not working.

"Well," he thought, "the show must go on." He rose slowly
and stylishly, walking toward center stage; only slightly
dragging his left leg behind, hoping the stain wouldn't be
too noticeable.

Bradley suddenly realized he was also feeling anxious. He
hadn't felt anxious (or so he liked to believe) for as long as
he could remember. In fact, he had made a solemn vow
many years ago to never sweat. It had cost him a small
fortune in antiperspirants, but it had been worth it. Yet
now, here, he was actually nervous.

Narcissistic and insensitive as he was and cool and collected as he liked to think he was, he had just watched others like himself get taken down by this kid who was probably descended from alien immigrants, a kid who obviously had little money or success yet had incredible power anyway. Bradley associated money with power. It was an obvious correlation that didn't seem to matter here. The proof was that no one seemed to care about his suit.

He closed his eyes and struggled in his mind for the right words. In his anxiety, he actually began to pray for guidance. Much to his surprise he began to quote verses from the Bible previously avoided. He opened his eyes, held out his hands and spoke to the audience:

"When you pray, you are not to be like the hypocrites; for they love to stand and pray in the football stadiums and on the television so that they may be seen by men. Truly I say to you, they have their reward in full.

But you, when you pray, go into your inner room, close your door and pray to your Father who is in secret, and your Father who sees what is done in secret will reward you.

And when you are praying, do not use meaningless repetition as the pretenders do, for they suppose that they will be heard for their many words. So do not be like them; for your Father knows what you need before you ask Him."

Paul looked up at him with disbelief.

Bradley turned towards Jesus and continued:

"Young man, I have no questions for you, nor will I stand here and try to discredit you. I have been a hypocrite, a liar and a con-man. I am ashamed of myself. I have used God and Jesus as valets and I could not go into my inner room because I had filled it with new clothes!"

"I have learned from you that we are all indeed God's sons and daughters, equal in His Eyes and Heart, yet you are a better son than I and richer for it. I was poor as a child and I decided that riches meant money, yet I am so poor compared to you."

Bradley walked over to Jesus, who stood to meet him. He bowed his head before Jesus and said, "My brother, I will do better now. Thank you."

Jesus, feeling a deep, brotherly love for this man, put his hand on his shoulder and simply nodded his understanding.

Everyone in the audience looked at his or her neighbor and felt the same connection, siblings all, sibling rivalry gone.

Bradley stood up tall, returned to his seat and sat down.

Paul went over to Bradley and licked the stain on his trousers. It disappeared! Bradley was both relieved and amazed!

Paul, also amazed, started thinking of ways he and Bradley might market his Magic Saliva Stain Remover. *"I'll talk to him about it after the show,"* he mused.

Miracles and money are not necessarily irreconcilable.

"Well, we have one panelist left," began Pontius as soon as everyone was resettled in their appointed places, "and there's no telling where this one will take us! I have to admit, this show is nothing like I imagined it." He stood up and gestured to the audience, like a rock star pumping up the crowd. "What do you think? Has this been fantastic or what?"

The crowd all stood up and cheered. They began chanting "Jesus, Jesus, we all love Jesus!"

Jesus put his fingers to his lips, quietly asking for silence. The chanting trailed off into that place where sounds disappear.

Pontius began again. "Our last panelist is the lovely and devout televangelist and wife of our stylish ex-televangelist. Please welcome the inquiries of Mrs. Bambi Nation."

To everyone's surprise, it was Jesus who stood and approached Bambi, who was sitting thoughtfully on her chair, wondering what to do. Like her husband Bradley, she was at a loss for words. She had hitched her wagon to her husband's agenda and it had been very lucrative. He was good at selling salvation and their marriage lent certain legitimacy to the whole Christian American Dream of the very rich and successful holy family with God as their provider Who arranged their perfect life with intimate and intricate detail thing. It was their success and wealth that attracted others. It was their wealth that inspired others to believe in their special connection with God, to accept them as God's intermediaries and messengers. It was their wealth and success that everyone wanted and came to get. "In God we trust" was written on money, for God's sake, and only an idiot would believe that Americans would worship a God that measured wealth in terms other than financial. In this culture, no one would follow a poor person, or believed a poor person could possibly know the will of God. In this culture everyone wanted to be the beneficiary of the Will of God! Shit, even the Popes always sat their rich, fat asses on golden thrones!

But in her heart, Bambi knew it was all an act. She and Bradley knew that the people wanted to belong, to feel good about themselves, to feel that God (or anybody for that matter) loved them, to be among the chosen like Tuday a few seats over, and they would give their trust and money to the ones who could present the most convincing show. Oh, it wasn't all a scam. Singing and praying side by side with thousands like themselves, congratulating each other for making the Right Choice, convincing each other that this was The Way really did feel good, better than anything had felt before. But Bambi had known for a long time that they had no special conduit to Divinity, they didn't really have any more direct experience of God than anyone else. She was usually more concerned with her makeup, hair and wardrobe than she was with God. Bradley certainly spent more time worshipping in the privacy of his closet trying on his suits than he did thinking about God, unless of course he admitted that money was his God.

"And your hair and how you look is important," Jesus said to her. "It's part of how you were created, it's part of being human, man or woman. I suspect God cares about looks, too!"

Bambi looked up, startled by Jesus' comment, startled that he knew what she was thinking. She blushed with embarrassment, feeling exposed, vulnerable. The thought, *"This show is called Exposed and so we are,"* flashed in her mind.

"Would you like to dance," Jesus asked, hand extended?

Pontius jumped up indignantly. "Now hold on, this is not Dancing with the Stars…"

"Grrrh."

Pontius looked down. Paul was chewing on his pants leg, dragging him back to his seat.

"What the hell," he complained as he shook his foot free.

Paul growled and stood his ground. Pontius grumbled and sat back down.

"Here? Now?" Bambi shyly asked.

"Please."

Suddenly, John Lennon's song, "Woman" began playing and Jesus and Bambi began dancing. The audience all stood and began to sing along.

"Woman…

As they danced and the audience sang, they talked.

"This is your planet, you know," Jesus said.

"What do you mean?" Bambi asked.

"This planet is a beautiful woman, and you are part of her consciousness. She enjoys and desires the presence of the masculine energy, but only men who honor and love her, protect her and care for her. You, like your Mother, should only allow such men in your life."

"Bradley has always been good to me."

"Yes, I can see that. He treats you well and has given you much, but you must take the lead because the future of this planet depends on women like you taking positions of leadership, with their men in supporting roles. This has been difficult to accomplish because most of the men on this planet are not followers of the local Mother but followers of an invading God."

"Invading God? Are you serious or are you pulling my leg."

"I'm serious, and it's Paul who's pulling on your leg."

Paul had joined the dance. Jesus looked down and signaled to Paul with his eyes to let go and go back to his place.

"Yes, I am referring to the God described in the Old Testament, who wasn't God in the absolute sense, but a rather uptight, narcissistic control freak sort of guy. Think about it. He commanded his 'chosen' people to 'have no other gods before him.' That means there were other gods he was jealous of and in competition with. He also had penis issues."

"Penis issues?" Bambi tried to stifle a laugh.

"It's OK to laugh. It's really quite funny. Yes, penis issues. He commanded his people to mutilate the penises of all the male children eight days after they were born. I would call it tribe branding and very weird and controlling. What a sweet guy, yes! Women were not allowed at the bris, nor did they ever want to watch. If they did they would probably have put a stop to the practice, not wanting to see their son's pain, not seeing the need for it."

"Oh, and that's not all; he tested his 'people's' loyalty and subservience to him. He wanted Abraham to prove his obedience by sacrificing his son Isaac. He wanted Abe to kill Ike to prove his love. That's kind of sick, don't you think? The foreskin of the penis became the symbol of the sacrifice of the son."

"Well, when you put it like that, yes, it is kind of sick."

"Seems to me like a very insecure kind of god."

"Women, mothers," Jesus continued, "would never put up with fathers sacrificing their sons, even if some so-called god commanded them to do it, unless they were brainwashed, cowed and media molded into believing the same crap. And that's how it is. Look at all the religious wars. It's the same crap. The fathers send their kids off to kill and be killed (sacrifice and be sacrificed) to defend some religious bullshit, to satisfy some phony god's death

156

wishes. And the women, most of them anyway, waving flags, believing in their Abrahams. At least Abraham was bailed out at the last minute by an angel (probably an angel that knew about the particular god's warped and sick sense of humor). Today's Abrahams, today's tribal (national) leaders, don't pull back the knife."

"We've been duped, haven't we?" Bambi asked.

"Yup. duped in the names of God and Jesus and country. People even believe that God Himself sacrificed His own son Jesus because He loved his people so much. Would you really be inclined to worship a God who had his own son killed? I sure wouldn't."

"No, not really. I should do something, shouldn't I?"

"Yup again."

"Thanks, I'll give it some serious thought. I'll talk it over with Brad. He's always been open to my input and he's really a teddy bear, very supportive. He's been duped, too."

"Yes, he's a good man. I expect you will do fine things for this planet and I'm sure he'll be with you all the way. Thanks for the dance," Jesus said as they circled over towards Bradley. Jesus bowed to her and kissed her hand. He gave a 'you're a lucky guy' look to Bradley and returned to his seat. Paul gave him a 'that wasn't fair' look, sighed and lay his head on the floor.

Pontius stood before his throne and looked seriously at the audience. Then he cast his royal glance at Jesus.

"Will the defend...er, Jesus, will you please stand to receive the closing statements from our panel of 'experts.'"

"Cardinal Cluck, your closing statements please."

Cluck rose from his red seat and walked to the center of the stage. He seemed taller and thinner as he had untelescoped himself. Jello-like no more, his presence was both lighter and more confident, softer and stronger, brighter and full of eager anticipation.

Facing Jesus, he recited one line:

> "The sanctification of repression
> Inevitably begets obsession."

Smiling, he put his palms together in prayer position, bowed his head and returned to a standing position in front of his seat. He would never let Jesus stand alone again.

Pastor Tuday didn't wait for Pontius to acknowledge him. He rose and also approached Jesus.

> "The very idea of elitist exclusion
> Qualifies for the darkest delusion.
> We who are by hatred driven,
> Forgiven are by Belonging's Given."

He put his hand on Jesus' heart and Jesus responded in kind. Their eyes met in mutual understanding.

In harmony they simultaneously said: "I am honored to be on Team Life with you."

158

Then they did a fist to fist salute followed by a high five. Timothy went and stood with Cluck, both smiling, both transformed.

Bradley rose and came forward, putting his hand up to silence Pontius' protests at being ignored and bypassed as master of ceremonies.

Stylishly he spoke.

> "Religious rationale of greed is never a good deed.
> It benefits no one to take more than they need."

Bradley bowed and shook hands with Jesus. They both placed their hands on the other's shoulder. Bradley then turned and joined the others.

Jesus walked over to Bambi and offered his hand. Bambi accepted it and stood.

She held his hand as she spoke her closing remarks.

> "The vilification of Eve
> We no longer will believe.
> Of the sinfulness of Woman,
> We have only been deceived.
> This Earth is Woman Wise
> Never again a conquered prize!"

She leaned close, kissed his cheek and whispered, "You are an incredibly hot young man. Thanks for the Dance." She joined her husband, took his hand and gave him a playful, sexy kiss. Bradley's stylish suit shifted accordingly.

Suddenly, seemingly from out of nowhere, the Rasta Man reappeared with a microphone in His Hand.

"There is no power in weapons and war mon. Weapons cause pain and suffering, weapons kill. Where is the power in that, mon? The power is in the music. Music is how we celebrate life. Womon and Mon, I present to you the heavenly music of Sibling Revelry!" Then He disappeared in His cloud of smoke.

A curtain that wasn't there before went up. Jesus stood there with his guitar together with Luke on the bass, Marcus on the fiddle and Maria Magdalena striking up the rhythm on her drums. Rasta Man appeared again playing the trumpet. Jesus and Maria doing vocal, began their closing statement, a song of Peace.

"Open your hearts to the lives around you, your sisters and your brothers,
Take away the doubt and fear that keep you feeling lonely.
Live in the Peace of the trust and love, in the Peace of the One Great Spirit
Sing with us a joyous song of Peace."

Miraculously, the words of the chorus were floating in the air for all to see. Full of glee, the audience all joined in and belted out the verse.

"Peace, Peace, Peace, I can hear all voices singing
Weaving in the winds through forests and through towns.
Peace, Peace, Peace, I see all the people dancing,
Dance and sing for Planetary Peace."

Luke soloed the next verse.

"Hate and fear will darken hearts and darken the world we live in
From our songs of Peace, darkness will withdraw.
Bless the day, bless the way, bless the ones around us
Sing with us a joyous song of Peace."

Then the audience again sounded the chorus, so stoked it was a wonder they all didn't just leave their bodies, sprout wings and float up to the ceiling!

"Peace, Peace, Peace, I can hear all voices singing
Weaving in the winds through forests and through towns.
Peace, Peace, Peace, I see all the people dancing,
Dance and sing for Planetary Peace."

Marcus continued.

"When others fight, profess their might and fill the world with worry,
Sing to them of Peace, dispelling all their fears.
Dance in the sun, play, have fun, sing of Peace and Plenty,
Sing with us a joyous song of Peace."

And Maria, in her rich, powerful, heartfelt voice, sang out the last verse.

"We'll cleanse our world of hate and fear and join with the friends around us,
With our peaceful smiles we'll welcome one and all.

We'll work, we'll play, we'll dance all day the Dance of
the Peaceful Spirit
Sing with us a joyous song of Peace."

The audience, bouncing up and down, arms in the air,
singing at the top of their lungs, joined the Revelry once
more with the chorus. The horn of the Rasta Man vibrated
absolutely every cell in the universe with His trumpet call
of Peace. God, He was having fun!

"Peace, Peace, Peace, I can hear all voices singing
Weaving in the winds through forests and through towns.
Peace, Peace, Peace, I see all the people dancing,
Dance and sing for Planetary Peace,
Dance and sing for Planetary Peace."

Joy was palpable, impregnating every cell of every body.
The words, "the power is in the music, mon," resounded in
each person's mind.

The curtain that wasn't there before went down and
everyone went back to their seats except for Pontius who
approached the audience.

"We have heard from our esteemed guests and witnessed
some strange, powerful and wonderful things here on
Exposed. Now it is time for you, the people, to judg…, er
weigh in and express your opinions."

Pontius turned, looked up and signaled with a raised hand.
A large dial descended towards the back of the stage,
coming to rest above and behind the participants. Across
the top, in red, neon letters was the word, "Fraudometer."

162

To the far left of the dial was the phrase, 'Phony Baloney,' to the far right was written, "The Real Thing." Directly above an arrow pointing straight up in the center it read "No One Really Cares."

"If you think this discussion was a waste of time and you would have rather had a beer and watched a ball game, do not clap at all and the arrow will stay pointed towards 'No One Really Cares'. If you believe our vict…, er guest Jesus here," Pontius turned and waved his hand towards Jesus, "is a fraud, clap loudly when you are prompted to vote for fraud. By the way, the definition of a fraud is: some one engaged in deceit, trickery, sharp practice, or breach of confidence, perpetrated for profit or to gain some unfair or dishonest advantage." If, however, you believe from your experience here on Exposed that Jesus has been genuine and honest in his presentations and responses, with no deceitful agenda, express yourselves noisily when the choice for 'The Real Thing' is presented."

"Now, it's time to vote. Once the votes have been counted, the decision is final and Jesus will either leave triumphantly with many new followers or alone in rejection and shame."

Pontius walked back and stood below the huge dial of the Fraudometer. He was very proud of this part as it was his idea and invention. Beneath each voting prompt was a microphone that measured the audience noise level, tipping the arrow towards the choice that was turned on when that vote was called for. Expecting and desiring a particular outcome, he had inserted a more sensitive microphone beneath the Phony Baloney prompt. He was going to do the same under the 'No One Really Cares' prompt too, as a

163

backup in case his guest had some credibility, but one of his assistants told him it wouldn't matter since no one was going to make any noise if that was their choice. He wasn't quite convinced and didn't understand fully, but he let it go. Pontius didn't feel any hesitation as regards his desire to exert some control over the proceedings because it was his show, and because the Fraudometer was his invention and he knew best about these things.

"The time has come," he projected dramatically. He raised his hand and pointed to the left. 'Phony Baloney' lit up bright red. "Those of you who think Jesus is a fraud, let the world know!"

The silence was broken briefly by a burst of applause and some whoops and hollers towards the very back of the audience. A small group of a dozen men or so who all looked strangely like the actor Adrian Brody had jumped up and applauded, pushing the arrow weakly towards the red letters on the left. The rest of the audience turned silently and menacingly towards them and they quickly grew quiet, sheepishly lowering their heads and sitting down.

The arrow returned to the No One Really Cares position.

Pontius now pointed towards the right. The Real Thing lit up bright green and the audience went totally bonkers with loud, joyful clapping, foot stamping, hooting and hollering. "Jesus is the Real Thing, Jesus is the Real Thing," could be heard, via satellite television, all around the world. The arrow lurched to the right, jammed in position under the green letters. The chanting continued with people dancing in the aisles, hugging and kissing each other.

On stage, all the 'experts' were giving Jesus a standing ovation and Paul, head raised to the sky, was howling with delight. Even Pontius was dancing happily, mostly because he had been informed through his ear piece that the show's ratings had set new records!

Sibling Revelry, still on stage after performing Jesus' closing statement, picked up their instruments and began the intro to The Youngbloods hit, Love One Another Right Now. Jesus and Maria moved close together, singing a duet and everyone in the theater joined in, wondering how they knew all the words to a song not sung for forty years. Even Paul howled in tune.

Pontius felt something wet drop on his head.

A white dove hovered over the singing couple's head.

The curtain came down and the audience, some singing, some still chanting the name of Jesus, filed joyfully out into the night.

Chapter 18: Lamentation

Mal and his cronies, in the rear of the audience and still disguised as Jews, were fuming at the show's outcome. Their faces were red-hot with anger, looking rather ridiculous because the latex noses they were wearing remained a pale flesh color. The effect was somewhat like an unknown species of proboscis monkey and the people in the audience near them were looking at them strangely. It was not at all going as he and Pontius had planned. Instead of this Jesus guy being shamed and ridiculed on national television, he came out like some kind of Hero; a psychological miracle worker injecting truth, sanity and accountability into the minds of the panel and the theater and television audiences. The Fraudometer had exploded on the side of Authenticity from the audience and e-mail responses. Even Pontius, who with Mal, was counting on successfully disgracing Jesus and fanning the fires of hate to increase ratings and sponsorship (his motives, unlike Mal's, were about money and not personal) was ecstatic at the outcome. He didn't care if Jesus had won or lost, only that the show would go on. In fact, the show was a smashing success, audience participation was record-breaking and he had already been notified via the telephone insert in his ear that sponsors were clamoring for ad time for the next show. Pontius' Pilot would go down in television history as a milestone in media communications. He had created a world-changing show; his place in history was assured.

The people around Mal and his white-nosed thugs, suspecting something weird about their looks and acutely aware that this little group was the only one that clapped

166

for Fraud during the voting, began shouting and pointing in their direction. At the sudden attention, Mal thought it best to leave quickly. He and his gang jumped over the rear seats and ran out the back door. On their way out, they passed Judas who looked at them scornfully and triumphantly.

"Who's the real betrayer," Judas thought, and feeling good inside, walked out into the night humming his favorite Dylan song, finally understanding his mother's faith that he was on God's side.

"That Hispanic bastard won't get away with this," was what Mal was thinking as he ran into the night.

Jesus, with Paul at his heels, had retreated to the dressing room where his make-up was being removed. Maria Magdalena, his mother Maria (Jose' didn't like crowds and was watching it on TV with his cows), and the rest of his gang joined him. They were all talking excitedly about the show's outcome.

Pontius strutted into the dressing room with a huge grin on his face. He looked at everyone and waited for all to turn toward him with full attention before speaking.

"It didn't turn out as planned, but it was the most watched pilot ever produced! Our sponsors are clamoring for ad space and our producer has scheduled time for a whole year! Sixty Minutes, move over, Pontius has arrived!"

Then he turned toward Jesus. "You were very good. The people like you, the sponsors like you and the producers like you. In fact," and here Pontius paused for effect, "they asked me to put together a new show, with you as the star, called 'Coming Home to Jesus!'"

"What do you think? This is an incredible opportunity. You could do miracles, straighten out people's lives, sooo much better than Dr. Phil!"

Jesus looked up at Pontius. He was speechless.

"I know, too much too fast. Let's let this first success seep in and we can talk later. I'll go and tell your agent, Judas is his name right, about all this and he can get with you to arrange everything." Pontius swept out the door as quickly and as full of himself as he entered.

Jesus was quiet, feeling that it was all still wrong somehow, feeling sad at how far from sanity the people of this planet were and how easily their minds were changed.

While his friends and family were congratulating themselves, and Paul was eagerly soliciting scratches and pets, Jesus quietly rose from his chair and walked outside to get some fresh air. He looked up at the moon and wondered what his Father was doing. He was feeling sad, lonely and homesick.

He stepped off the curb and into the street. Behind him, he heard the squealing of a car burning rubber and the angry roar of an engine fully accelerating. He turned, and in the instant before the car hit him, he saw the glaring eyes and ghoulish grins of some strange creatures that had very red faces and large white noses.

Jesus' body was badly mangled and there was blood everywhere. He looked down at what was left of his body, shivered at the sight, and said, "Why have You forsaken me?"

"E tu Jesu?" A voice responded.

"What?"

"It's Latin. It means 'you, too.' I give everyone life and when some other guy kills them, I get blamed! Why me? How can You do this to me?! Actually I expected better from you."

Jesus looked to his left. A young, strong and very beautiful man stood next to him dressed in women's clothing. His hair was long and black and He wore a very sexy, black velvet evening gown. Pearls adorned His neck and hung from His ears.

"Dad?" asked Jesus, suddenly feeling a deep, incomprehensible and illogical joy. "Why are you dressed in drag?"

"God, by definition, includes all possibilities son. You know we can't let petty human beliefs and opinions limit the possibilities of creation. And women's panties feel sexy and open me to what women feel when making love! Mmm, You should try it sometime."

Jesus, always surprised by his father's behavior, thought about black lace and Maria and felt a rise between his legs. Then he looked over at his body and remembered what had just happened.

"Do you really think I would forsake you? Did you really want to take that job as a talk show host and get caught up in saving people? They'll work it all out, eventually."

"Did you notice that you're not really dead?"

Jesus looked at his body and realized that the body was over there while he was over here. He was also feeling pretty good.

"No one ever dies," God waved his beautifully manicured hand dismissively, "only their physical body loses its usefulness sooner or later. It's like an all terrain vehicle that gets worse for wear and has to be traded in for a new model. Yours over there is definitely totaled! Pity though. It was relatively new, and one of my finer designs! Oh well, dust to dust as they say."

"Hey," God in Drag continued, changing the subject, "I caught your show; very impressive and enjoyable; hope you didn't mind my little cameo appearances. You know me, it's hard to resist making an occasional, dramatic gesture."

"I especially look forward to seeing Cluck's transformations. You didn't really want that show, did you?"

"No, not really. That's why I came out here by myself, because what went down in there didn't feel completely right. What's next for me?" Jesus asked.

"Well, you seem to be finished here. Not much you can do with what's left of that. Go back into it to say your goodbyes and final words of wisdom and I'll meet you by the pool when you're finished."

God then walked down the dark alley, hips swaying and muttering to Himself about not quite getting the right rhythm. Then he disappeared.

Jesus shot back into his mangled body at the same time his friends, mother and lover ran out of the theater after hearing the car noises and the sound of the impact. Paul ran out, tail between his legs and began to howl sorrowfully at the moon.

Maria Magdalena ran to Jesus and fell to the ground next to him. She lifted his head calling his name over and over again without making a sound. Her voice wouldn't come out. Her heart was imploding and she couldn't breath.

Jesus' mother knelt next to her son across from Magdalena, picked up his limp hand and held it between her own. Tears were running down her cheeks and she was filled with a silent grief. Deep in her heart there was stillness, a knowing that what had happened was inevitable and had happened before. In her love she bent over his bloody body, took his face in her hands and kissed him.

171

He awoke and looked into his mother's eyes. Then he turned and looked into the eyes of his lover. Softly, he spoke to his beloved Marias.

"I am so sorry," he said to them, "so sorry that I cannot stay and love you longer. I am sorry my pain and my leaving will cause you grief."

"No," Magdalena protested, feeling panicky now that Jesus was conscious. "No, I'll get help, you don't have to go," and she started to yell at the others to call for help.

Jesus painfully held up his hand for her to stop and beckoned her to come back to him.

"Stay with me, Maria. Let our last moments here together be just for us."

Maria turned back to him and, with tears in her eyes, put her hand on his cheek and spoke to him.

"Jesus, Jesus, Jesus, my sweet and gentle and magnificent man." No more words would come, only tears.

"Listen carefully," Jesus whispered. "Live your life from your heart and do whatever you can to bring all our Father's children together. You know we all come from Life's Spirit and Womb. You know we are all eternally one Being, but our brothers and sisters feel separate, left out and alone. Hold everyone you meet in your heart and embrace them in your arms until they feel like they belong. No one needs be saved from anything but their belief in their aloneness."

172

"Don't preach to anyone and don't create anymore religions around what I or anyone else has ever said or done. Just care for each other. Like John Lennon imagined, 'and no religion too.'"

"If someone asks about Jesus, just tell them he was a fine man and a gentle lover, and make sure no one wears little cars around their necks to commemorate how I died this time. I can just see all the new necklaces of cars with crosses on them. Some will even begin holding services in cars and parking lots, reenacting the Running Over of Jesus!" Jesus' eyes filled with laughter as he said this and both Marias smiled even as their hearts continued to ache with a sorrow as deep and pulsing as the sea.

Jesus then called all his friends to him and called all the others who had since gathered around him, including the reporters with their microphones and cameras. He looked around at them, his eyes filled with a peace and a love none would soon forget.

He spoke to Everyone.

"This Jesus thing you are all so invested in has been a huge mistake built on lies and false promises. Jesus never came here to save anyone. He came here to live a life of love and responsibility, based on the truth that we all come from the same Being and we are all One Family. If you believe he came as a messiah to save people, then he has to be remembered either as history's greatest failure or the future's false hope! One look at the way you have messed up the world will confirm his failure. In truth, it is your failure, not his. If you accept that he came not as a savior

173

but as a brother to remind us of our Father and our Divine Heritage, then for you, his life was his gift, his life was *for giving.*"

"I, too, am Jesus. I, too, came to love and be loved, not to save or be saved. It's simple really."

"The man who mangled this body with his car knew what he was doing. He will listen to what I say on the news later and to him I say thanks for the ticket back home. I don't die, nor do I need resurrection. I leave this once strong and sexy body behind, having used it well."

"It is past time for this whole Jesus thing to be over. It's been going on for two thousand years and enough is enough. Every year brings a renewal of the suffering, every year someone uses the suffering and false promises to line his pockets and steal from others."

"You will all reap what you sow. Jesus is gone. You say you love him? Well then, let go of him; let him finally rest in peace as you would anyone you have loved and lost. When he left the last time, he told his disciples and everyone else through them to call on the Holy Spirit for help and guidance. She is in the hearts of all living things, infused in every atom of Creation. You can access and depend on Her, whatever names She is given, whatever faith you follow. Paramatma, Kuan Yin, Shekina, Tara, White Buffalo Woman, The Holy Dove; you just call out her name and you know wherever you are She'll come running! You got a Friend. Grow up. Good bye."

Jesus looked again into the eyes of his dos Marias, smiled and whispered "Hasta la vista, we are eternally in Life together." Then he left his mangled body behind.

Paul whimpered, crawled between the Marias and laid his head on Jesus' breast.

Chapter 19: Return to Margueritaville

Jesus found himself sitting by the pool at the right hand of God with a cool, fresh marguerita in his right hand. God, again in His Form as Zeus, also had a Marguerita in His right hand.

They looked at each other, held up their glasses and smiled.

"Welcome Home, son," God said as he leaned over to watch the aftermath of Jesus' death in the pool. "Looky here."

An ambulance had arrived and removed the body. The two Marias and Jesus' friends had gathered and were comforting each other while Paul began to sniff the tire tracks on the street. He then took off down the road, nose in the air, running as fast as his four tiny legs could move his oversized body. Everyone, including the policemen who recently arrived tried to keep up with the floppy-eared, barking Bassett.

As they watched in the pool, Paul, barking and growling furiously, led them to a car that had smashed into a streetlamp. The policemen ran up and pulled the dazed and confused men with strange, large white noses out of the wreck. The driver's white nose had somehow come loose and was pushed up over his eyes; his real nose bashed and broken on the steering wheel. All of them had little skull caps pinned to their heads. He was muttering something about immigration and how the country was being ruined by Jews and aliens and that no one knew how to pronounce Jesus' name properly anymore.

Jesus and God looked at each other and totally cracked up. They laughed so hard that the figures in the pool looked around fearfully as a 5.5 earthquake shook Southern California.

When they stopped laughing, they looked at each other with deep sorrow in their eyes.

"I failed, again, didn't I Father?"

"No, son, you didn't," God acknowledged. "There wasn't a whole lot more you could have done. Even the first time around you couldn't do much. Hell, you gave a few good sermons, healed a few people and then went and got yourself killed! It was your followers who did all the rest of this messy business and put all their energy into remaking the world to satisfy their own wants; fitting the world into their own belief systems instead of fitting themselves into the real world. 'Seek and you shall find,' I said. That means if you seek miracles, you find miracles, look for trouble and you find trouble. It doesn't mean that any of it is necessarily real."

"What about that 'Knock and it shall be opened,' what did you mean by that?"

"Oh, I just said that for the kids for when they went trick or treating on Halloween."

"You didn't fail. It wasn't up to you, then or now. Remember what Bob Dylan, that skinny guy with the boyish facial hair back in the sixties, said: 'There's no success like failure, and failure is no success at all.'"

177

"What did he mean by that?" Jesus asked.

"I'm not really sure," God responded with a grin, "but it sounded good. They said a lot of things back then that sounded good, even if they were incomprehensible."

"Then who is responsible for all this, You?"

"I suppose I can be given both the credit and the blame, but that's just a cop-out, the one most often taken. 'Why hast Thou forsaken me, Yada, yada, yada. We're all responsible, all creators. There's no beginning or end to creation. It just Is. 'Never was there a time when I did not exist, nor you, nor all these kings.' That's a quote from another good book used to create a number of cults. That's what's so wonderful about creativity; we never know what will happen. It's always full of surprises. It changes and flows and transforms as we think and dream and act, sometimes pleasant, sometimes horrible, always wonder-full and mysterious."

"In other words," Jesus said, feeling great joy in just Being, "We make our beds and then we have to lie in them."

"Precisely."

They toasted each other once more and drained their glasses. The Father put His arm around His son and they walked off together, disappearing into that place that isn't a place, where everyone came from and will surely return, and… live happily ever after.

Amen.

Chapter 20: Paul's Close Call

Paul, after being chased away by the policemen for chewing on the driver's leg, was looking for Maria Magdalena. He scampered down the street in his dog body, tail between his legs, feeling pretty low. (Bassett hounds usually felt low, because they are, but this time he felt **really** low). He knew that life had done one of those radical turns and things would be very different. Yet he also knew History continued on because of and in spite of his delusional and/or lucid contributions. Jesus, once again, had set things straight enough for them to go crooked again and this time he got to hang with him in person, without having to fabricate a visionary experience. Thinking this, he felt better and his tail rose up wagging.

As he sauntered around the corner, nose vacuuming up the smells gathered in the canine library that is the crack where wall meets street, he heard an awesome, blaring sound, like celestial trumpets. He looked up, startled, into a glaring, blinding light and went totally blind!

"Oh, shit! Not again," he thought, as he instinctively backed away from the light. He closed his eyes tight and when he opened them again he could see. What he saw sent chills of terror through him, setting the hairs on his back up in waves. There, behind the bright light was a truck with the words "Animal Control" written in huge letters.

Paul turned and ran, tail between his legs, both frightened and relieved.

"No more world influencing visions (delusions) for me," he thought.

Safe from the dog catcher, he sidled up to a fire hydrant for some blissful relief.

"It's the simple pleasures that really count," he mused, "and besides, every story has to have a male pee scene."

Epilogue: Where everyone goes

Maria, Jesus' mother, went home to Jose'. They became
foster parents and lived out their lives in peace. Jesus
visited them often, though they could not see him.

Maria Magdalena took Paul and moved to the Best Friends
Animal Shelter in Utah, where they both met new lovers.
They became ardent animal rights activists.

Judas got a contract with Neil Young as a publicist for his
anti-war concert tours.

Bradley Doe Nation gave up his ministry and had Paul's
saliva synthesized. He made millions with the stain
remover and bankrolled Bambi's bid for the Presidency of
the United States. He created a trust fund for Paul and made
sizeable contributions to Best Friends. He still wore very
stylish suits but created a small altar and place to pray in
his closets.

Timothy "take me away" Tuday became a little league
coach. He made sure no kid was left behind and everyone
got to play.

Pontius went on to produce many more pilots, becoming
richer and more and more obsessive. He eventually
developed a nervous disorder and looked like he was
always washing his hands.

Cardinal Cluck left his order and went on the Subway Diet.
He lost 150 pounds and fell in love with a woman named
Mary. They took up Tantra and facilitated sexuality

workshops. They also produced and starred in some very tasteful, erotic movies, had two kids and lived happily ever after.

Mal was convicted of drunk and reckless driving and manslaughter. After saying he was sorry and promising to convert to Judaic Hispanicism, he was freed on parole and sentenced to do agricultural work at an orange grove owned by Melvin and Gladys Friedman.

As for everything else in the world, well, you're here, you know how it is.

Appendix A:

Prior predictions and wishful thinking as regards the end of the world:

The following is a partial list gleaned from http://www.armageddononline.org/failed_armageddon5.php

You can visit their website for a more extensive list which is still probably missing thousands of other catastrophic predictions that never happened. I predict that at the end of this list there is a special opportunity for you!

AD 156 A man named Montanus declared himself to be the "Spirit of Truth," the personification of the Holy Spirit, mentioned in the Gospel of John, who was to reveal all truth. Montanus quickly gathered followers, including a pair of far-seeing "prophetesses", who claimed to have visions and ecstatic experiences supposedly from God. They began to spread what they called "The Third Testament, a series of revelatory messages which foretold of the soon-coming Kingdom of God and "The New Jerusalem," which was about to descend from heaven to land in Montanus' city of Pepuza, in Phrygia (modern-day Turkey), where it would be home for all "true" believers. The word was spread, and all were urged to come to Phrygia to await the Second Coming. The movement divided Christians into two camps, even after the New Jerusalem didn't appear. Whole communities were fragmented, and continuous discord resulted. Finally, in AD 431, the Council of Ephesus condemned Chiliasm, or belief in the Millennium, as a dangerous superstition, and Montanus was declared to be a heretic. Despite the failure of the prediction, the cult survived several centuries until it was ordered exterminated by Pope Leo I. --SSA pg 54

AD 380, The Donatists, a North African Christian sect, predicted the world would end in 380.

AD 387 St. Ambrose, Bishop of Milan, identified the Goths with Ezekial's Gog. The Goths had just destroyed the Imperial army at Adrianople, prompting Ambrose to say, "...the end of the world is coming upon us." --TEOTW pg 27

AD 300 St. Martin, Bishop of Tours: "Non est dubium, quin antichristus...There is no doubt that the Antichrist has already been born. Firmly established already in his early years, he will, after reaching maturity, achieve supreme power." --TEOTW pg 27

AD 500 At the mid-fifth century, Vandal invasions recalled calculations that the world would end in the year 500, 6000 years after Creation, and spurred new calculations to show that the name of the Vandal king Genseric represented 666: the number of the Beast. --Apoc pg 34

AD 500 Hippolytus of Rome, a third-century theologian supported the oft-accepted (for the day) view of the end of the world occurring sometime around the year AD 500. He used a mass of scriptural evidence, including the dimensions of the ark of the covenant. --TIME pg 31

AD 590 Bishop Gregory of Tours, who died in AD 594, calculated the Time of the End for sometime between 799 and 806. --Apoc pg 48

Ad 848 The Christian prophetess Thiota predicted the world would end in 848.

AD 970 Lotharingian computists foresaw the End on Friday, March 25, 970, when the Annunciation and Good Friday fell on the same day. They believed that it was on this day that Adam was created, Isaac was sacrificed, the Red Sea was parted, Jesus was conceived, and Jesus was crucified.

AD 992 A rumor that the end would come when the feast of the Annunciation coincided with Good Friday. This happened in 992, when Easter fell on March 22, and eager calculators established that the world would end before three years had passed. --Apoc pg 50-51

AD 1000 Christian authority all over the known world predicted the second coming in the year 1000.

AD 1033 When the world did not end in 1000, the same Christian authorities claimed they had forgotten to add in the length of Jesus' life and revised the prediction to 1033. The writings of the Burgundian monk Radulfus Glaber described a rash of mass hysterias during the period from 1000-1033.

AD 1033 The roads to Jerusalem fill up with an unprecedented number of pilgrims. Asked why this is happening, the 'more truthful of that time...cautiously responded that it presaged nothing else but the coming of the Lost One, the Antichrist, who, according to divine authority, stands ready to come at the end of the age." -- TIME pg 47

185

AD 1100 Guibert of Nagent (1064-1125) informed would-be crusaders that they should seize Jerusalem as a necessary prelude to its eventual capture by Antichrist. "The end of the world is already near!" he explained. --TIME pg 61-62

AD 1184 Various Christian prophets predicted the end of the world in the year 1184. Nobody seems to remember just why.

AD 1260 A Dominican monk named Brother Arnold gained a following when he wrote that the end was about to take place. According to his scenario, he would call upon Christ, in the name of the poor, to judge the Church leaders, including the Pope. Christ would then appear in judgment, revealing the Pope to be the heralded Antichrist. --SSA pg 56

AD 1284 Pope Innocent III predicted the end of the world in the year 1284, 666 years after the founding of Islam.

AD 1300 A Frenchman, Jean de Roquetaillade, published a guide to the tribulation. Imprisoned for most of his adult life, he predicted Antichrist in 1366, to be followed in 1369 or 1370 by a millennial Sabbath. Jerusalem, under a Jewish king, would become the center of the world. --Apoc pg 55

AD 1348 Agnolo di Tura, called "the Fat," writing during the time of the Black Death: "And I...buried my five children with my own hands, and so did many others likewise...And nobody wept no matter what his loss because almost everyone expected death... People said and believed, 'This is the end of the world.'" --TEOTW pg 115

AD 1349 The group known as the Flagellants claimed that
their movement must last thirty-three and a half years,
culminating in the Second Coming. They persuaded many
people that their assertions were true. One chronicle states:
"Many persons, and even young children, were soon
bidding farewell to the world, some with prayers, others
with praises on their lips." --TEOTW 125-129

AD 1420 Martinek Hauska, near Prague, led a following of
priests to announce the soon Second Coming of Christ.
They warned everyone to flee to the mountains because
between February 1 and February 14, 1420, god was to
destroy every town with Holy Fire, thus beginning the
Millennium. Hauska's band then went on a rampage to
"purify the earth", ridding the world of, in their eyes, false
clergymen in the Church. They occupied an abandoned
fortress which was named Tabor, and defied the religious
powers of the day, ultimately succumbing to the
Bohemians in 1452 --SSA pg 56, TIME pg 75-77

AD 1490 Girolamo Savonarola, a Dominican visionary,
attracted large crowds with his prophecies of Antichrist. He
began preaching that his city of Florence would soon be
"The reformation of all Italy..." and that its people would
take on the mantle of God's elect, saved from destruction to
play a glorious new role. This would only be accomplished,
however, if Florence submitted peacefully to the invading
Charles VIII of France. They did so, and for a short time
became what has been called a 'proto-Messianic republic.'
But when the corrupt Pope Alexander VI regained
Florence, Savanarola was publicly executed in May, 1498.

--TIME pg 79-81

AD 1500 Martin Luther, Protestant reformer, stated: "I persuade myself verily, that the day of judgment will not be absent full three hundred years. God will not, cannot, suffer this world much longer... the great day is drawing near in which the kingdom of abominations shall be overthrown."

AD 1500 The Italian artist Botticelli captioned his painting, "The Mystical Nativity" with a message warning that the end of the world would occur within three years, based on the predictions of Girolamo Savonarola.

AD 1526 Anabaptists in St. Gallen, Switzerland, excited by various leaders and events, began running through the streets and shouting that the Last Day would arrive in exactly one week. Many were baptized, stopped work, abandoned their homes and set off into the hills, singing and praying in expectant fervor. After a week had passed with no sign of their returning Lord, they returned to their homes. --TEOTW pg 145-153

AD 1520 Nicholas Storch was a former weaver who was a self-proclaimed expert on the Bible. He began warning groups of workers that all of Christendom was about to be annihilated by the Turks. Not only did he quote from the Scriptures, but insisted that God spoke to him directly through dreams and visions. Ultimately rejected by reformer Martin Luther, Storch vanishes from history at the end of 1522. --TEOTW pg 155

AD 1520 Thomas Muntzer, another self-appointed prophet in Germany, who made bold predictions based upon the book of Daniel, and called for the overthrow by the peasantry of those in power. "The time of the harvest is at hand," he declared. "...I have sharpened my sickle." Muntzer proclaimed that it was the Last Days, and whoever resisted his preaching would be, "..slain by the Turks when they come next year." He was executed in 1525, after leading a peasant army in rebellion. TEOTW pg 153-158

AD 1520 Melchior Hoffman (c1498-1543/4) was one of the most influential of the self-appointed prophets. A Swabian furrier by trade, Hoffman had converted to Lutheranism in 1522 and became a wandering preacher. In 1526 Hoffman published a detailed pamphlet on the twelfth chapter of Daniel which proclaimed that the world would end in seven years, at Easter of 1533. The seven year period was to be divided into two parts. The first part would see the appearance of Elijah and Enoch, who would overthrow the Pope. They would, however, be martyred and all the saints would then be persecuted. After forty-two months of tribulation, Christ would appear. Hoffman referred to himself as Elijah, and embarked on the fulfillment of his vision. He was imprisoned for his views, however, in Strasburg, later dying in the 1540s. --TEOTW pg 160-162

AD 1527 A German bookbinder named Hans Nut said that he was a prophet of God sent by Christ to herald the Second Coming. This would occur exactly three and a half years after the start of the Peasant's War, in 1527. The Lord's arrival would be followed, according to Nut, by a thousand years of free food, love, and free sex. He amassed some followers, but was killed during an attempted prison escape in 1527. --SSA pg 56

189

AD 1532 Bishop Frederick Nausea (yes, that is his name), predicted that the world would end in 1532 after hearing a single report of bloody crosses appearing in the sky alongside a comet.

AD 1533 Anabaptist prophet Melchior Hoffman predicted the end of the world in 1533. He also predicted that Jesus would reappear in Strasbourg, to save 144,000 people from the world's end.

AD 1532 Michael Stiefel, mathematician and follower of Luther, published Apocalypse on the Apocalypse: A Little Book of Arithmetic about the Antichrist which computed the Day of Judgment for 8AM on October 9, 1533. when nothing happened on that day, the local peasants seized the minister and took him to nearby Wittenburg, where some sued him for damages. Stiefel survived this misadventure and, twenty years later, published a "recalculation." --Apoc pg 91-92

AD 1555 French theologian Pierre d'Ailly predicted the end of the world in 1555. Christopher Columbus' own apocalyptic views were based on this prediction.

AD 1583 Several astrologers and clergy cite a conjunction of Jupiter with Saturn as a sign that the second coming of Jesus will occur in London at noon on Apr 28, 1583.

AD 1584 Above prophecy is revised one year later.

AD 1594 John Napier, mathematician extraordinaire, published A Plaine Discoverie of the Whole Revelation of St. John, in which he predicted the Last Judgment either for

1688, according to Revelation, or 1700, according to
Daniel. --Apoc pg 92

AD 1600 Martin Luther predicted that the world would end
no later than the year 1600.

AD 1624 The same astrologers who failed in predicting a
great flood in 1524, finally moved their predictions safely
beyond their own deaths, to 1624.

AD 1648 Sabbatai Zevi, a rabbi from Smyrna, Turkey,
predicted that the Messiah would come in 1648. When
1648 arrived, Zevi announced that he was the Messiah.

AD 1656 The date the world would end, according to
predictions put forth by Christopher Columbus in his
"Book of Prophecies". Columbus held that his explorations
were fulfillment of prophecy. he was to have led a
Christian army in a great final crusade that would
eventually convert the entire world to Christendom. The
date was chosen because supposedly 1656 years passed
between the time of the creation and Noah's flood. --99R pg
13

AD 1657 The Fifth Monarchy Men, a group of radical
Christians intending to force the British Parliament to base
all laws on the Bible (much like Christians are trying to do
to the United States) predicted the world would end in
1657.

AD 1666 Few believe Rabi Sabbatai Zevi is the Messiah,
so he changes his prediction for the appearance of the
Messiah to 1666. He is arrested for disturbing the peace

with his prophecies, and when given the choice between execution and conversion to Islam, eagerly converts.

AD 1688 John Napier, the mathematician who discovered logarithms, applies his new mathematics to the Book of Revelations and predicts the end of the world for 1688.

AD 1694 Anglican rector John Mason and German theologian Johann Alsted both predict the end of the world for 1694. Another German prophet Johann Jacob Zimmerman, predicted that Jesus would reappear in America and organized an expedition of Christians to sail across the Atlantic and welcome their savior when he reappeared. Although Zimmerman himself died on the day of departure, his followers completed the journey and remained encamped in the wilderness of North America until it became obvious that Jesus had stood them up.

AD 1700 Jonathan Edwards, premier evangelist, was fascinated by the Apocalypse, noted all signs of the times, and calculated and recalculated its coming. He concluded that Antichrist's rule would end when the papacy ended in 1866, and that old serpent, the Devil, would finally be vanquished in the year 2000, when the Millennium would begin. --Apoc pg 171

AD 1700 Sir Isaac Newton, the great scientist, was himself not immune to misprophecy. He developed a carefully constructed grand scenario which predicted that the Jews would return to reclaim Jerusalem in 1899, and that the second coming of Christ would occur precisely forty-nine years later.

AD 1800 Mother Ann Lee, leader of the "Shaker" movement, claimed that in her the female principle of Christ was manifested, and the promise of the Second Coming fulfilled. Christ's kingdom on earth, according to Lee, began with the establishment of the Shaker Church.

AD 1832 Mormon founder Joseph Smith prophesied under "divine revelation" the gathering of the saints and the coming of the New Jerusalem, the temple of which would be built in Missouri and "reared in this generation." Smith added "Pestilence, hail, famine, and earthquake will sweep the wicked of this generation from off the face of the land, to open and prepare the way for the return of the lost tribes of Israel from the north country....there are those now living upon the earth whose eyes shall not be closed in death until they see all these things which I have spoken, fulfilled." --99R pg 120

AD 1840 Dr. John Cumming, eloquent preacher of apocalypse, drew audiences of many thousands to his lectures. Cumming, while preparing for the publications of these lectures, warned that the seventh and final vial of God's wrath was now being poured out. "We are about to enter on the Last Woe...and to hear the nearly-spent reverberations of the Last Trumpet." --TSOR pg 84

AD 1844 William Miller, a Massachusetts farmer, after a years-long study of the Bible, chiefly Revelation and Daniel, concurred that the Second Coming of Christ would take place between 21 March, 1843, and 21 March, 1844. When this time passed, Miller and his followers set up new dates, again with failure. Eventually the movement collapsed, but gave birth to Seventh Day Adventism, while also influencing the formation of several others, including the Jehovah's Witnesses. --SSA pg 58, TSOR pg 16, Doom pg 92-111

AD 1850 Chinese schoolteacher Hung Hsiu-ch'uan, failing a government job examination for the thrid time, suffered an emotional collapse during which he professed to have had visions of an old man in a golden beard, as well as a younger man. These two told Hung that the world was overrun by demons and that he, Hung, was to be the instrument in their eradication. Later, after returning to his home village, Hung reread a Chinese Christian missionary's book and discovered the meaning for the vision which he had experienced. The old man had been God, and the younger man, Jesus. Hung further understood that he was the second Son of God, sent to save China. Eventually his charisma and teachings began to gather a following and he became the leader of a group known as the Pai Shang-ti Hui (God Worshipper's Society). By 1850 the movement had grown into open rebellion. In 1851 Hung proclaimed the new dynasty the T'ai-p'ing T'ien-kun (Heavenly Kingdom of Great Peace), and assumed the title of Heavenly King. His ragtag group of thousands grew into a disciplined army of over a million. Full scale war erupted across the Chinese countryside. Chinese imperial troops were defeated in pitched battle on more than one occasion. Hung captured the city of Nanking, making it his capital. Eventually he fell ill, and committed suicide in 1864. Chinese forces lay siege to Nanking, and in taking it inflicted a terrible slaughter of over 100,000 people. The rebellion gradually faded across China. As many as 20,000,000 people died as a result of this, the T'ai-p'ing Rebellion, and Hung Hsiu-ch'uan's misprophetic delusions.

--Brit 1977, vol 8

AD 1870 Cyrus Read Teed, a former corporal in the Union medical corps, said that he was the "seventh messenger of God", and adopted "Koresh" as his new surname. Teed claimed that an angel had visited him, giving him new spiritual awareness. He was now the reincarnated Messiah, and it was his job to gather the 144,000 faithful to await the Last Judgment. Teed's legacy would bear bitter fruit in the 1990s, with the rise of another Koresh, David, who would lead his followers into an apocalyptic death near Waco, Texas.

AD 1874 Charles Taze Russell, founder of what would become the Jehovah's Witnesses, first announced that the Last Days had definitely begun in 1874, then that the end would come in 1914. Succeeding Witnesses placed the date in 1925, 1936, 1953, 1973... --99R pg 20

AD 1890 A native American known as Kicking Bear claimed to have received a certain divine revelation. Christ had returned to earth, given his followers a new spiritual magic, the "Ghost Dance", which they were to engage in until Christ came again to "take them up into the air," eventually to be set down among the ghosts of their ancestors on the new earth, where only Indians would live. The movement spread quickly among the various tribes on and off the reservations, especially among the Sioux. -- Bury pg 431-435

AD 1901 In 1889, the Rev. Michael Baxter, editor of the London Christian Herald, announced in a book called The End of This Age about the End of This Century that 1896 would witness the Rapture of 144,000 devout Christians, and that the world would end in 1901. --TIME pg 120-121

AD 1918 Clarence Larkin, in his book Dispensational Truth, writes, "...at no time in the history of the Christian Church have the conditions necessary to the Lord's return been so completely fulfilled as at the present time, therefore his coming is imminent, and will not probably be long delayed...If the Millennium is to be ushered in in AD 2000, then the "Rapture" must take place at least 7 years before that...It may have been 4075 years, instead of 4004 (as generally given) from Adam to Christ. In that case we are living in the year 5993 from the creation of Adam, or on the eve of the Rapture." --Disp

AD 1973 The "Children of God" cult claimed that its leader, David Berg, was "God's end-time prophet to the world." They fled America in 1973 due to Berg's prediction that Comet Kohoutek would destroy the country. --99R pg 117

AD 1976 Prophecy teacher Doug Clark announced that President Jimmy Carter would be "the president who will meet Mr. 666 (the Antichrist) SOON!" A flier announcing Clark's new book that year claimed, "The Death of the United States and the Birth of One World Government under President Carter." --SSA pg 24 (Personal note: I was working at a TV station in Orange County California whose manager believed the Clark prediction, and transformed the station's output into 24 hour a day warnings of the end of the Earth, even to the point of abandoning the commercials rotation. The Earth did not end but the TV station went out of business.)

AD 1980 Prophecy promoter Charles Taylor predicted a 1988 rapture: "This new book (Watch 1988 - The Year of Climax) is being written with the expectation that it will be the last book I will ever write ...with the millennial reign of Christ due to begin in 1995, the rapture must surely occur in 1988 to coordinate with many other prophecies!" Not surprisingly, Taylor also made similar predictions for 1975, 1976, 1980, 1982, 1983, 1985, 1986, 1987, and, of course, 1989. --SSA pg 134-142

AD 1981 May 25. About fifty members of a group called the Assembly of Yahweh gathered at Coney Island, NY, in white robes, awaiting their "Rapture" from a world about to be destroyed between 3PM and sundown. A small crowd of onlookers watched and waited for something to happen. The members chanted prayers to the beat of bongo drums until sunset. The end did not come.

AD 1988 Edgar C. Whisenant, in his book 88 Reasons Why the Rapture Will Be in 1988, gave a three day period in September for the saints to be "caught up with the Lord." When this failed, he issued another book claiming that he was a year off, and urging everyone to be ready in 1989. -- SSA pg 28-33, DOOM pg 134

AD 1991 Reginald Dunlop, end-times author, stated that "The Antichrist would be revealed" around the year 1989 or 1990, perhaps sooner." The Rapture he predicted for 1991. Says Dunlop, God verified this "through many prayers...I am MORE than positive that this is THE YEAR that the Rapture will occur." --SSA pg 36

197

AD 1992 "Rapture, October 28, 1992, Jesus is coming in the Air." Full page add in the October 20, 1991, issue of USA Today, placed by followers of the Hyoo-go (Rapture) movement, a loose collection of Korean "end-times" sects. When the prophesied events failed to pass, much turmoil broke out among the sects. Some believers were distraught, while others tried to attack their doomsday preachers with knives. The founder of one church was later charged with swindling four million dollars from his parishioners. --99R pg 11, 168-169

AD 1993 David Koresh, self-proclaimed little lamb of Isaiah 16, and the Second Coming of Christ, dies in a fiery conflagration with some 80 of his followers. These members of the Branch Dividians, an offshoot of the Seventh-Day Adventists had faced a botched ATF raid on their compound near Waco, Texas, and a subsequent 51-day siege by the FBI. A devastating fire broke out when the FBI attempted to fire gas into the group's buildings. --99R pg 122-124

Bibliography (What the abbreviations mean)
Thief = Thief in the Night by William Sears, George Ronald press, 1977
99R = 99 Reasons Why No One Knows When Christ Will Return by B.J. Oropeza, InterVarsity Press, 1994
SSA = Soothsayers of the Second Advent by William M. Alnor, Fleming H. Revell Company, 1989
Doom = Doomsday Delusions by C. Marvin Pate and Calvin B Haines, Jr., InterVarsity Press, 1995
TEOT = The End of Time by Damian Thompson, University Press of New England, 1996
Armada = The Armada by Garrett Mattingly, Houghton Mifflin Company, 1959
DISP = Dispensational Truth by Clarence Larkin, Rev. Clarence Larkin Est - publisher, 1918

Apoc = Apocalypses by Eugen Weber, Harvard University Press, 1999
Bury = Bury My Heart at Wounded Knee by Dee Brown, Holt,
Rinehart & Winston, 1970
TSOR = The Sleep of Reason by Derek Jarrett, Harper and Row, 1989
TEOTW = The End of the World by Otto Friedrich, Coward, McCann
& Geoghegan, 1982
Hand = Handbook of Denominations in the United States - New Eighth
Edition by Frank S. Mead, Abingdon Press, 1985
Brit = Encyclopaedia Brittanica

As predicted at the beginning of this appendix, you are all
in for an unexpected opportunity. Now it is up to you to
predict the future. Just fill in the blanks in the sentence
below and you can join all the above seers and become part
of history that never happens; or…will your predictions
actually come true? What do you wish for?

I_____your name here_____, of the esteemed
order of_____your church or cult or place of employment here_____, in the
glorious country known as_____, do
prophesy that the world will_____what do you think the world
will do?_____, on the _____day of
_____month_____, in the year_____. My advice to all
humankind on the day of this prophesy is to_____.
(Add extra pages if necessary).

Good Luck!

ABOUT THE AUTHOR
LUIGI ENRICO PIETRA D'ORO

Luigi Enrico Pietra d'Oro currently teaches art and art history at a small, rural community college in Southern California where he spends a lot of time encouraging his students to question what they believe and think for themselves. He has taught art, primarily sculpture and ceramics, for over 35 years to all age groups from kids in Kindergarten to senior citizens.

He has traveled extensively and taught sculpture workshops in Brazil, American Samoa, Italy, Germany, England, Switzerland, Australia, New Zealand, Canada and Hawaii.

Luigi has studied and practiced numerous spiritual disciplines and has first hand knowledge of fanaticism. He doesn't recommend it.